The House on

Apple Blossom Lane

© 2024

infiniteofone.com

Published 9.11.24
by
Infinite of One Publishing

Chapter 1

Duncan Mills had never thought much about what his father, Jonathan Mills, did for a living. He knew he was a lawyer, of course. He also knew that he exhibited a seemingly incompatible combination of sweetness and ambition. And he must be good at what he does considering where they lived and where his older brother and sister go to school on the East Coast, with his father footing the bill for all of it. So he felt gratitude towards his father for his generous provisions made on behalf of the family. Otherwise, he had no real thoughts or strong feelings about his father's profession.

He'd been to his office in downtown Seattle a few times. His father had named his business after himself. Mills and Associates, LLP, it's called. The five story building in which it's housed is nondescript, overshadowed by most of the edifices surrounding and looming far above it, many dozens of stories high, as though making the statement that the businesses that they contain and the businessmen that run them will always tower far above his father and his endeavors. Occupying the top floor as one of ten businesses in the building, the office is quite snug and simply appointed. Mills and Associates, LLP fields five lawyers, including his father, all of whom share one secretary.

Then comes the fateful Thursday during his senior year of high school. It's nearing spring, and the flowers beginning to bloom only seems to magnify the bloom of Samantha Conway. She races around his head all the time. Those big hazel eyes. That curly brown hair. That infectious laugh. The way everything she says is emphasized with gesticulation, as if words aren't enough and she needs her hands to express the entirety of her excitement. He'd watch this gestured enthusiasm from afar, wishing he was one of the 'cool kids' close enough to know what she was describing. His constant thoughts of her make him fear that he has an obsessive in him, and he's long associated obsessiveness with illness.

His sister Anne used to obsess a lot, about a great many things. Eventually she was diagnosed with obsessive compulsive personality disorder. She'd even been briefly hospitalized once, shortly after the death of his mother. That was the start of it. She couldn't let it go. She suffered what seemed to be a series of panic attacks and relentlessly questioned their father about every little detail of that fateful trip that ended her life. But, eventually, with medication, she'd seemed to get over it, and was now studying law at Yale, as their father had.

"You may *be* a bit obsessive," his father's girlfriend, Marie, had said to him when Duncan had shared his fears with her of going down the same road as his sister. "But don't

   The House on Apple Blossom Lane

worry, your father is too. And I think that it's the very thing that makes him so good at what he does. In fact, I'd say it's near impossible to be anywhere close to the best without having that personality trait. Because if you don't obsess, you're unlikely to get anywhere near to the best results. It's simply the price to be paid if you want to be one of the best at what you do. That *includes* loving, I think. Obsession and passion are practically synonymous; they're side effects of loving fully. The key is learning to apply that obsessiveness to healthy loves and progressive pursuits, always looking forward rather than ruminating on the past or, worse, having that obsessiveness mislead you towards self-destructive habits. *That's* what I worry about when it comes to your father. That he'll end up... diving into the wrong sea."

Marie is a local yoga instructor. Eerily, she's near the spitting image of his deceased mother, almost as if his dad was looking for her doppelgänger, or like God himself had taken pity upon him and sent a mirror image, with bright blue eyes, blonde hair and the same svelte figure as his mother. She's wiry, and often speaks of her love of yoga and Tai Chi. But in contrast with both his steadfast father and deceased, restless mother, her manner couldn't be more different. She's almost always mild-mannered. Seemingly the perpetually detached observer, she possesses an almost supernatural, steely stoicism. Duncan senses something unusual about her, like she's hiding her true self; like she's concealing a great reservoir of strength that's being belied by her soft-spoken manner.

According to his father, he'd met Marie at a bar shortly after burying his mother. His father had told him a little about their odd, melancholy courtship. He'd been drinking too much that night, as was common back then. His father had convinced himself that he was inconsolable, until she approached him and did exactly that; console him. He'd said she was compassionate and patient beyond

 The House on Apple Blossom Lane

words, and that she'd demonstrated the rarest of qualities: a complete capacity for listening.

Within a month she'd moved in. Their relationship became so serious so fast that Jonathan, his father, worried that Duncan might be offended; like it was disrespectful of his deceased mother. Jonathan worried that Duncan might think that he was betraying their mother by becoming so seriously involved with someone so near to her death. But that's not how Duncan felt.

Since his mother Darla had been killed two years before, just prior to his sister Anne's breakdown, swift recovery and, six months later, her joining his brother Tom at Yale, Marie's been his father's rock, lending support that he felt allowed his father to carry on, keep his job and avoid the mental derailment suffered by his sister. She'd become a stabilizing force, coming in to counter his family's instability at just the right time, and not just on behalf of his father. So he's very appreciative of her, even feeling indebted to her. His mother had been a pharmaceutical chemist, and was much like his father, so busy and driven, with her mind remaining at work, that he found it difficult to sit her down and talk to her. Marie is different. She's easy to talk to, about anything.

Duncan consistently surprises himself with how open he is with her, and was from the start. Telling her about Samantha. About how he thinks of her while lying in bed at night. Not in a sexual way, but with an overwhelming longing to have *anything* to do with her. He tells her about how nervous he's always been around girls, and how envious he is that his brother always found it so easy.

Though he and his brother Tom look alike, with 'the body compositions of athletes contrasting with the countenance of accountants,' as his mother had often said, a

     The House on Apple Blossom Lane

full, thick head of wavy red hair set atop a round, fully-freckled face, all placed atop the build of a volleyball or water pollo player, Duncan always felt like his brother carried it better. Maybe it was the fact that Tom could actually grow a beard. He, on the other hand, couldn't decide which was worse, that he hadn't been able to grow facial hair until he was seventeen or that it was somehow a different color than his head hair, dark brown. 'God has a sense of humor,' he'd say to himself. He wanted so badly to finally find the same confidence as Tom so that he could make Samantha his first girlfriend. But he had some serious competition there: a whole slew of students that were athletes head to toe.

Samantha seemed to be in the process of being actively pursued by half the guys at school, including the captain of the football team, Jake Holloway, and a bunch of other guys on the football team. The football team was well known, having come within a game of going to the state championship the year before. That success had garnered them a great deal of popularity in the Seattle area, and something close to lore in local circles. And Samantha is a fan. She isn't a groupie or anything, but he can tell that she doesn't mind their attention.

So Duncan finds it hard to believe when, upon leaving his chemistry class, he runs into Samantha and Jake fighting in the hallway. And it isn't a little argument, either. Her face is red and she appears on the verge of tears. She's holding what looks to be a Valentine's Day card in her hand. She yells "No!" and tries to get away from him, but he grabs her by the arm and says: "Let me explain! I didn't mean it that way!" But Samantha clearly isn't interested in his explanation. She's jerking her body away from him while moving in Duncan's direction.

Duncan thinks: 'This is my chance.' He moves quickly towards the two of them as Samantha rips herself away from Jake again, and when

Jake reaches for her arm once more Duncan steps boldly between them.

"She said no, asshole!," Duncan shouts. "Why don't you leave her alone? You think being the big football captain makes you entitled to everything? To *everyone*? It's hard to believe that everyone doesn't bow down to the great Jake Holloway, isn't it? That all the girls don't throw themselves at you! You just can't take hearing *no*!"

Samantha, still upset and seemingly embarrassed by the attention the squabble is generating from the other students, gives Duncan an odd look, then puts her head down and scampers off. That's when Jake looks Duncan in the eyes with a look that he'll never forget; like Jake really *sees* him for the first time, and is overcome with incredulity at the audacity of his intervention. The look of shock and disbelief fast fades, however, and is immediately replaced with a look of seething contempt.

"Oh yea, *asshole*?," Jake says, coming within inches of his face. "Well at least my father isn't some lowlife gangster! How many killers has your father gotten out of doing time this year alone, you piece of shit?"

Duncan is sure that he's about to be in his first fight, making it hard to focus on the accusations being leveled. 'This can't end well,' he thinks to himself, expecting to be shoved to the ground at any moment. Instead, standing eye to eye with Duncan, menacing him, Jake fumes for a few seconds before, amongst the gathering crowd, another football player, the running back, Duncan thinks, breaks through and uses all of his strength to pull Jake back. Hand on Jake's chest, he whispers something in his ear, and the expression on Jake's face reverses course from fury to something closer to terror.

Duncan, unable to take his eyes off of Jake, overwhelmed by the complete and sudden

 The House on Apple Blossom Lane

change in Jake's demeanor, is shocked when Jake suddenly manages a "sorry" before putting his head down and allowing himself to be pulled away by the running back and another teammate, both of whom shoot Duncan a series of backwards glances before disappearing into the fast-dispersing crowd.

'What the hell just happened?,' Duncan thinks to himself.

The next period Duncan is in class with a girl he believes to be the running back's girlfriend, seeing them hanging around together during every lunch break. During a lull in some group work he gets up the courage to approach her. "May I speak with you for a minute?," he asks, before leading her to a corner of the classroom.

Duncan isn't even sure she'll follow, and expects her to be annoyed, if anything. But, instead, she looks worried, and follows him immediately while looking around to see who's watching. 'This is one of the popular girls,' Duncan thinks. 'I was expecting her to act irritated or supercilious, not scared. What in the hell is going on?'

"You're with the running back of the football team, right?"

"Michael? Yes, well, kind of… we aren't really…"

"It's okay," Duncan interjects. "But something very strange happened earlier. And I need to know why. I don't really know how to ask this, but… does your boyfriend… like… *know* something about me?"

The girl's eyes dart back and forth, first reading Duncan's face, then surveying the rest of the classroom, then falling back onto his countenance. She's carefully measuring her reaction. She doesn't know what to say.

"It's okay," he tries to reassure her. "You won't get in trouble. And I swear to God that I won't say anything to anyone about this. I just need to know…"

"All I know," she finally whispers, "is that Michael's dad works for the government, and that…"

"Yes?"

"And that he told Michael to steer clear of you, and Michael told me the same, okay? Please don't tell him I told you that, okay? *Please*."

"Don't worry," Duncan manages after a moment. "I won't… My name's Duncan by the way."

"I know… I'm Alice."

The remainder of the day Duncan's head spins. He avoids everyone and everything,

including his schoolwork. His obsessiveness
has moved from Samantha to his father. He's
just a lawyer, isn't he..?

Duncan begins to think of events from his
past in a new light. He hadn't thought much
of them at the time, like they were just a part
of his dad's job as an attorney. But now he
can't help but wonder: Were these *abnormal*
occurrences? Were they suspicious,
somehow? The occasional phone calls and
knocks on the door in the middle of the night.
The furtive little sneak-away-to-a-corner-of-
the-house meetings during family parties,
held away from most of the family members,
when he'd been asked to entertain a dozen
kids while his father met with their fathers,
his mother serving martinis and gossiping
with the wives so perfunctorily, like she was
just doing her duty. How often his father was
'out of town.'

And then there was that trip to Greece and
Italy that summer before his mother was

killed, when a limo seemed to mirror them wherever they went, to his father's apparent surprise, with the driver saying "compliments of Mr. C" before dropping them off at prepaid outings all over Athens, and then Rome. He'd hear that abbreviated name many times thereafter, when gifts would come to the house, or whispered by his father to his mother. It could only be his father's boss.

Duncan had never thought much of it. He'd just figured that his father had wealthy clients, and that 'Mr. C.' was one of them. There must be a lot of lawyers that met whenever their clients needed them, and that showed their appreciation for their services with free meals and trips to NFL and MLB games, and nights at the opera.

But now he's suspicious. He begins imagining that his father works for a gangster. Or that, like Jake said, maybe he *is* a gangster. He has images from *The Godfather* and *Goodfellas* running through his head. 'My god, what is he, like a... what's the word, consiglieri, or something?' He has to know more; to know the truth.

So the next morning, after tossing and turning all night, Duncan gets up with the determination to know his father better. He's been on the outside for long enough; it's time for the inner circle. He imagines what he'll say to him when he confronts him at breakfast. 'It's okay Dad,' he'll tell him. 'You can trust me. I won't tell anyone anything. I just want to know what the family is involved in...' He heads downstairs earlier than usual to join his father and his girlfriend for breakfast.

Halfway down the stairs, Duncan hears his father's phone ring. Jonathan Mills is somewhere near the kitchen. Duncan freezes. He hears his father answer the phone, then walk towards his study. Duncan tiptoes down the stairs and sneaks towards the study. He presses his ear as close to the door to the

 The House on Apple Blossom Lane

study as he can, straining with all his might to hear, imaging his father has just been contacted by a real version of Don Corleone.

Duncan can't make out much. His father says something about an illness; about something needing to be examined further; about liability needing to be minimized by "developing alternative explanations." Then: "He needs to see me today? Can't you just send me the tape...? Fine. Well, I suppose that I can rearrange... At the house on Apple Blossom Lane? Okay, okay, tell him that I can be ready in thirty minutes."

Duncan runs as quietly as possible back up to his room, his head spinning with imaginings of some overlord living at a house on Apple Blossom Lane. Such an innocuous name for the street of a gangster's residence. Maybe that's the point. No one would imagine Don Corleone living in the Seattle suburbs on Apple Blossom Lane. 'How do I respond to this situation?,' he presses himself. 'I can't just go to school. I have to learn what I can.'

Using his map app, he looks up Apple Blossom Lane. It's well outside the city. A long road that starts out in the suburbs and leads to a school called Pacific Northwest Healthcare College before meandering through a number of large estates and ending up in a state park. There's no way to narrow down which house is being referred to. So he decides that the only way to find the house is to follow his father. But that'll be tricky. His dad knows his car, of course. How will he tail him?

Duncan hears his dad walk back up the stairs, and is fairly certain he pauses outside his door. He freezes, listening. He imagines his dad pressing his ear to the door, as he'd just done himself. 'Did he hear me lurking outside his study?' A few seconds later and he's fairly certain that his father has walked away. He waits another minute, then leaves his room and does his best ninja imitation, creeping towards his father's bedroom.

'I'm reduced to spying on my dad and his girlfriend… Why don't you just ask them about it, you pussy?,' he berates himself. 'Yea, *right*. Hey Dad, I suddenly have imaginings of you representing the mafia. Any truth to that?,' he scoffs, shaking his head. He envisions Marie having a heart attack and dropping dead on the spot. So, instead of knocking, he just listens. Nothing for a few minutes. He's about to sneak away when he hears Marie speak with an agitation that he's never heard from her.

"What? Today? I know they're important to your firm, sweetie, but I thought you'd changed your mind about those people? I swear Jonathan, if you're going to get in trouble for anything, it'll be because of *that* place. I *really* don't want you messing with those people anymore. I'm telling you, I have a really bad feeling."

"Shhhh!" his father forcefully whispers.

"They're going to get you killed, or thrown into prison. If anything you should be gathering evidence *against* them so that when they get indicted you have something to offer the government to protect yourself from facing the same. You really want your kids and I to be paying you visits in a federal penitentiary? Because *that's* where this is headed. No compensation is worth such a risk!"

"Are you insane Marie? Keep your voice down, please! Duncan will hear you!"

"He's not even awake! You're being paranoid again... and we both know why! Because they've made you think that *everyone* is being watched!"

Duncan hears someone move towards the door, and he darts towards his room,

     The House on Apple Blossom Lane

scampering across the hardwood floor. Just as he rounds the corner into his room, the door to his father's room opens. He closes his own bedroom door quietly, then turns off the light and sneaks into bed. A moment later his door opens. He hears nothing for a few seconds, feeling his father's presence looming in the doorway, then his voice:

"Shouldn't you be up and getting ready for school, Duncan?"

Pretending to be waking up, he stretches then rolls over and looks at his father. 'Who is this man?,' he wonders.

"What?," his father asks. "Why are you looking at me like that?"

He considers confronting him, but can't bring himself to do it. Instead, he plays dumb: "Like *what*, Dad?"

Jonathan Mills stares deep into his son's eyes with discerning suspicion. 'He knows I'm up to something,' Duncan thinks.

But his father says nothing about it, only: "Get up and get ready for school." And as his father walks away, Duncan makes his decision: 'I have to know about this house on Apple Blossom Lane. I can't ask him about it, because if he feels like he can't tell me about it, I'll just arouse his suspicions. So I'll have to follow him there.'

Duncan rushes through his morning preparations, showering quickly and shooting downstairs to scarf some breakfast so that he'll be ready in time to 'coincidentally' leave the house at the same time as his father. Normally the morning scene is calm. But this morning is different, and not just because of the thoughts and emotions brewing within him. Even Marie seems on edge, cursing when she accidentally lets some of the shells fall into the eggs. She hardly ever curses. And his father seems to be eyeing him more than usual, occasionally peering at him over his paper, sipping his coffee with deliberation.

No sooner are the eggs and hash browns down Duncan's gullet when the doorbell rings, surprising Duncan and startling Marie, who drops the pan that she's cleaning, jarringly clattering into the sink. 'Who could be here this early?,' Duncan wonders. 'The phone call...'

"Well, that's for me, I have to get going," his father announces, placing his coffee mug in the sink, kissing Marie on the cheek and hurriedly straightening his grey suit and shirt and black tie in the foyer mirror, checking his brown combed-back hair. The red hair came from Duncan's mother. Jonathan grabs his briefcase, having been set below the mirror, then opens the door to reveal a granite block of a man, in black suit and tie. He's at least six foot six and broad as a barn across the shoulders and forehead, making his father, who has some size himself, look positively tiny by comparison.

"Good morning, sir," the man flatly rumbles.

"Good morning, Mr. Romero. Shall we head out?"

"Of course, sir."

"I have to get going too," Duncan suddenly proclaims. "I'm… meeting a few guys to do some test preparation before school."

Jonathan Mills pauses briefly and shoots his son a look before exiting and closing the front door. 'He looked worried,' Duncan thinks before quickly thanking Marie for breakfast and dashing into the garage. He opens the garage door and starts his white Prius. 'I was expecting to follow my father's car. This may be more difficult…'

As Duncan backs quickly out of the garage, he's distressed to find that the only car on the street, what appears to be a black Lincoln Town Car, is already halfway down the block in the opposite direction from the way he normally goes to school. He frenziedly screeches into a turn and accelerates down the block, trying to keep the vehicle in his sight. To Duncan's surprise the Town Car turns the first corner, going deeper into the Eagle Crest Estates community.

'That's odd,' Duncan thinks, comparing the vehicle's course to the location he saw on the app. 'Shouldn't he be going straight there, toward the freeway?'

Duncan doubles his acceleration and makes the right turn five seconds later, then slams on his brakes, stopping in the middle of the road. There, parked at the curb on the right side of the street, set in the shade of a string of mature maples, is the black Town Car. A moment later his father opens the back left passenger door and walks over to Duncan's driver's side door. He's scowling, a look of dread on his reddened face. He motions for Duncan to roll down the window. There's no way out of the situation, so Duncan complies.

"What are you doing, Duncan?," his father asks, a slight tremble in his voice, as if trying to conceal his fear.

"I... I was going to get something to drink at Charlie's Market before going to school... but I saw you take the right and I was worried that you weren't paying attention and your driver was lost..."

"Duncan, listen to me very carefully," his father half-whispers, as if worried that the driver might overhear them. "Not everyone that I represent likes to be... *noticed*. Some people are *very* protective of their privacy, and pay me to help keep them out of the public eye. They pay me *not* be seen. Do you understand what I'm saying to you, son?"

"I... I think so. But Dad..."

"Not now, Duncan," his father cuts him off. "If you insist on asking me questions, you can ask me tonight when I get home from work. Now, do me a favor and turn around and go directly to school, okay?"

"Okay Dad."

Frazzled, Duncan does a three-point turn and heads towards school. He imagines Mr. Romero holding a gun to his father's head. Then pulling the trigger, and taking the cannoli. Fifteen minutes later he's parked in his school lot, in a daze. 'So Jake, Michael and Alice are right. My dad works for... what, the mafia? *There's no way...* What do I do? I can't just go to my classes and pretend like everything's okay all day. I know! I'll call his office and convince the secretary to give me the address!' He comes up with an excuse while trying in vain to remember the secretary's name. 'What was it..? Gretchen, maybe..? Something starting with a G...'

Scrolling through his contacts list on his cell phone, he finds the number for his father's office and places the call. It rings only once.

"Mills and Associates, Grace speaking, how may I help you?"

"Hello Grace, it's Duncan, Mr. Mills' son. Perhaps you remember me? I've been in to see you and my dad a few times..."

"Yes, of course Duncan. I actually knew you when you were just a little guy. You and my daughter used to play together. You were so cute. You probably don't remember. How are you today? If you're calling for your father, I'm afraid he isn't in the office at the moment."

"I know. Actually, he just called me. He needs me to drop off some important paperwork at the house on Apple Blossom Lane. But I forgot the exact address, would you mind telling it to me?"

A pregnant pause ensues, then: "I'm sorry, Duncan, but I'm not allowed to give out the addresses of clients. It violates attorney-client privilege. I'm sure you understand. Why don't you just call your father and ask him for the address?"

"I would, Grace, but, you see, he told me his phone was about to die when he called me, and now it's going straight to his voicemail." 'Please don't call him and call my bluff!,' he thinks during another extended pause.

"I'm sorry, Duncan, but I'm not allowed…"

"Please, Grace," Duncan adds a sense of urgency. "My dad says that it's really, *really* important. He said he could lose the client if he doesn't submit the paperwork today. He needs it signed ASAP."

Papers rustle, a few strikes of the keyboard, a heavy sigh, and finally: "6160 Apple Blossom Lane," she whispers. "You get that?"

"Yes, thank you Grace, you're a life saver!"

"But please don't…"

"Grace," Duncan hears another voice over the line. A male voice, likely one of the other attorneys, but he's not sure who. "Who are you talking to Grace?"

The line goes dead.

Chapter 2

Duncan types 6160 Apple Blossom Lane into the maps app on his phone. Zooming in on the app, it appears that the address places the house directly adjacent to Pacific Northwest Healthcare College, at the end of a two block line of houses bordering the campus.

'That's odd,' Duncan thinks. 'Wouldn't that make it, like, a house for college kids?' He thinks of his brother. How he likes to make him feel like his life is crap by comparison to his own. Tom told him recently that, in most collegiate communities, the surrounding houses act like drunken extensions of the campus, with most being rented by students. How that's part of why being a college student is *so* much better than being in high school and living with your parents. How, on the weekends, every other house has a keg in it, and there are gorgeous girls to flirt with lined up around the block.

If he's right, that makes it an odd place for a client of his father's to live. His imagination starts to spin again. Maybe it's like a secret society hiding within a frat? Or maybe it's a professor or school administrator? He imagines a tenured college professor using his position as a cover to conceal the fact that he's a CIA assassin. 'They call him *The Professor*,' he imagines. 'Failing *his* class is permanent... I'm watching too many movies,' he thinks to himself while heading towards the house.

It's a pleasant drive. A nice little slice of manicured suburbia. Large, well-kept lawns ringed by towering deciduous trees kept robust by the perpetual Washington precipitation. The biodiversity of the Pacific Northwest makes it an appealing place to live for anyone with an appreciation for natural splendor. His father assures him that rain is the necessary tradeoff if you want the endless hues of green calling every nature lover into the wilds beyond the city. It's astounding how many variations of green a healthy ecology can produce.

"Water is life," his father says. And even outside the emerald forests and the mighty mountains, in the midst of running rows of houses with overgrown laws, this truth is evident. Verdant hues run together as if one big yard; as if nature refuses to recognize the fences that man imposes upon its territories. Then, the college.

Entering the two blocks bordering the campus he's greeted by the large "Pacific Northwest Healthcare College" sign, appearing to have been carved into a cross-section of old growth redwood, followed shortly thereafter by the "College Way" invitation into the campus's central parking lot. It's not a particularly large school, yet it's quite striking to behold. With everything he's heard his self-described cynic of a sister say about the evils of conventional healthcare, it seems ironic to him that the school should sit in such an Eden.

Duncan catches a glimpse of the central grounds upon passing, with the administrative building positioned at the end of an extensive lawn, about half the size of a football field. Interspersed in the rich green is a multi-colored splotching of students enjoying the partly-cloudy cusp of spring. The building is framed in white, its roof supported by stately Corinthian columns.

About halfway down the second and final block bordering the campus, Duncan slows, knowing that he's nearing his 6160 destination. He realizes that he needs to approach with caution, so as not to spook anyone that may be watching. Every major gangster has guards on duty wherever they go, after all. Obviously you can't have someone barging into your home hidden in suburbia and shooting you in the head when you're trying to enjoy the spaghetti and meatballs with the family.

Adjacent to the home, both curbs are packed with cars. Again he thinks of his brother. How he says that the only way for most kids to afford to live next to campus is to cram together in the houses and share the rent, packing four or more students into every bedroom. He remembers how Tom told him that he and his friends had to stack a half-dozen kids into their sophomore spot, and that, in order to fit them all, that they built illegal bunks hanging from chains nailed into the beams of the ceiling in one large, raised-roof room, jokingly calling the space 'The Ewok Village' after the *Star Wars* scenes. He looks for the black Town Car, but there's no sign of it. Slowing to a crawl, he sees the house for the first time.

There's nothing special about it. That is, it doesn't stand out. It certainly doesn't appear

  The House on Apple Blossom Lane

to be anywhere that some head honcho would reside. It's not exactly the Nevada compound from the second *Godfather* film. Rather, it's a fairly typical looking two story white dwelling with navy blue trim, a ruddy wooden door and an American Flag. It looks similar to the other houses lining the lane, in fact, except that it appears newer, like it may've been recently repainted. The driveway is crammed with cars to an extent where no one near the garage is going anywhere without getting other cars to pull out of the driveway first. On the right side of the home is another driveway, far narrower, clear of cars and leading to what looks like a granny unit.

'There must be some mistake,' he thinks, coming to a stop in the middle of the lane while double and then triple-checking the address. 'Is this like pro bono work for a sorority or something? *Right*, Duncan, a sorority employing a muscle-bound freak picking up thousand-dollar-an-hour legal professionals for impromptu meetings... Maybe it's some tech whiz kid that invented the next Facebook, or, like, some Russian tycoon's kid that wants to slum it with the ordinary students and find out what it's like to fit in and be normal for a change.'

Sitting to the side of the road with nowhere to park, his little Prius quietly buzzing on idle, he suddenly feels the cost of over-stressing and not sleeping the night before, and thinks of his bed. 'This is ludicrous. What the hell am I doing here?' He glances at the clock in his car. 9:35 am. If he turns around now he can make it back to school in time for second period, minimizing the damage.

Yet something compels him to stay. The unsolved mystery of his father. 'Should I just go knock on the door? No, not with all that stuff my dad said about privacy and going straight to school.' Leaning his chair back a bit, he goes over all possible courses of action in his head, periodically glancing over at the house. He's about to nod off when the front door opens, startling him. Reflexively he releases his seat from the reclined position, shooting up. His first thought is that it's his father, and that he's in for a verbal thrashing. But it's not. It's just a girl, likely a student, wearing a backpack.

She heads off down the sidewalk towards College Way, paying him no mind. A moment later he notices in his rearview mirror that a car is pulling away from the curb a few car lengths behind him, on the same side of the street as the house. So, upon passing him, he decides to back up and take the spot, so he can watch for a while.

Upon parking he relaxes a bit, looking around more carefully. 'Damn my red hair,' he thinks whilst scanning the vicinity. 'I stand out like a sore thumb. Or more like a clown. I might as well be driving a miniature clown car.' That's when he notices that the house directly

across the street from 6160, 6161, has a sign
above the front door.

In large capital letters it reads: "TRACE."
Directly beneath: "Trauma Research and
Counseling Extension."

'A business? Something official, at least. *That*
must be where Dad is. Either Grace made a
mistake, or I heard her wrong.' Other than
the sign, the house looks almost identical to
6160, except that the trim is brown, not blue,
and there's no granny unit. 'Extension...
meaning that it's part of the college? I think
that's the word they use when universities
extend their services outside the main
campus. But if that *is* where Dad is, it's still
strange. It's not like a trauma counselor, or
any counselor, for that matter, needs a heavy
hitter like Dad.'

Duncan watches as earnestly as his energy
will allow. The TRACE home is quiet. Lights
are on inside, and a man with curly hair and a

　　The House on Apple Blossom Lane

goatee occasionally passes by the front windows, looking from the paper he's reading across the street to 6160 and back. In the surrounding homes more students exit, most heading towards College Way. No sign of his dad. No sign of anything interesting, frankly. Yet still, his instinct is to stay. Leaning his chair back again, he decides he's invested, and he'll wait for some sign of his father. Within minutes he falls fast asleep.

The slamming of a car door wakes him up, and he shoots up in his chair again. The left side of his head had been pressed against the headrest, a line of drool dripping down his cheek and pooling onto his shoulder. Wiping it away, he glances at the clock: 12:22pm. 'My God,' he thinks. 'I've been asleep for hours. Even if Dad *was* here, he's likely left by now. Some stakeout this is. It doesn't look like *detective* or *private investigator* are future job prospects.' This makes him think of investigation. 'I'll look TRACE up on my phone.'

The search query "TRACE" leads to many likely unrelated sites, so he searches by "Trauma Research and Counseling Extension" instead, and finds that the phrase is associated with universities all over the country, mostly technical and medical schools, especially on the 101 and I5 corridors of the west coast, from Southern to Northern California into Oregon and Washington. Clicking on the link for Pacific Northwest Healthcare College, Duncan finds that "TRACE" is the extension of "TRAC," "Trauma Research and Counseling," which appears to be both a program as well as a building at the college. At the top of the college's TRAC home page he clicks the link "The TRAC Foundation," leading to the page: "On TRAC: Giving back to the community since 2013."

The page reads: "The mission of The TRAC Foundation is to provide financial, academic and psychological support for trauma survivors nationwide. We offer housing, counseling and funding for trauma victims aspiring to earn their degrees, as well as program assistance for universities dedicated to better understanding and treating trauma." The banner beneath lists "Our Sponsors," a set of organizations funding The TRAC Foundation, many in pharmaceuticals and defense.

'Dad must represent one of those organizations,' Duncan thinks. 'Or maybe TRAC has nothing to do with why the kids at school think Dad is dangerous. Maybe it's just the pet project of some wealthy pharmaceutical exec that likes his privacy and feels safer with a big security guard. Shit! I've wasted my entire Friday!' He starts his car and is about to drive away when a knock on his window near stops his heart.

Turning to look, he's doubly surprised by the sudden materialization of Samantha, his crush. His heart erupting into his throat, he rolls down his window.

"Hi. It's Duncan, right?," she asks.

'She knows my name.' "Yes, that's right."

"What are you doing here?"

Duncan is unsure what to say, silently panicking.

"You here for the party?," she pulls him off the hook.

"The party?"

"Yea... Can you keep a secret, Duncan?"

"Sure."

"Some of us ditch part of school on Fridays sometimes and come here to see my sister and Michael's brother, Dan, and maybe have a few beers and smoke some weed. College kids like to start early on Fridays," she says with a cute little mischievous grin. "They live in that house right there," she adds while pointing at 6160.

'My God,' Duncan thinks. 'What are the chances of that? What the hell is going on?'

He hesitates. "Well, I…"

"Hey Sam," someone says on the sidewalk behind him. Poking his head out the window to look, he sees that it's Alice, walking next to Michael, the running back who'd kept yesterday's incident from becoming a brawl, coming in from somewhere behind him.

"What the?," Michael starts upon recognizing Duncan. "What the hell is *he* doing here?" They all look at Duncan.

"I… heard about the ditch parties here," he lies, grasping the lifeline Samantha threw him. "I thought it sounded cool."

"He shouldn't be here!," Michael blurts out. "No offense man," he says, addressing Duncan, "because I don't know you, but…"

"But what, Mike?," Samantha angrily asks. "Jake's cool to come whenever he wants, and so is your girlfriend, but not *him*?"

"It's not about being cool," Michael retorts. "It's…"

"What?," Samantha continues. "This rumor about his dad being dangerous? C'mon!"

"No, it's not that either. Not really. It's… I can't say."

"Well, he's coming in with me," Samantha replies while opening Duncan's car door and motioning for him to exit.

"Fine! Fuck!," Michael responds while shooting past Duncan as Duncan exists his Prius.

Alice, straggling behind Michael, asks: "Is your sister here, Sam?"

Samantha shoots her a hard look, then responds: "She isn't doing that anymore, *okay*? Besides, she's been ill lately, so you're not going to want to see her. She thinks it may be contagious."

Looking both embarrassed and disappointed, Alice hurries past them and catches up to Michael.

Samantha wraps her arm around Duncan's, so naturally that the titillation gives him chills. She slowly walks him towards the house.

"What is your sister doing?," Duncan can't help but ask, adding "if you don't mind my asking" when he sees Samantha's discomfort.

Samantha pauses, considering what to say, then responds: "My sister has... been through a lot. She was raped by a group of guys at our high school a few years ago. You may've heard about it."

"That was your sister?" Duncan recalls the story, but not the name of the girl. A pretty cheerleader, some say the prettiest girl in school, was roofied at the homecoming dance. A guy dropped something in her punch, apparently, then led her out of the gym where the school dance was being held, telling her he needed to talk to her about something. As the sedative set in, he forced her into the men's bathroom down the hallway, where three of his friends were waiting. She was conscious, but too weak and out of it to effectively resist as the four seniors sexually assaulted her. Ever since then the punch is no more, the overseeing staff has doubled and the leadup to every school dance includes an assembly with warnings to women of what to look out for, and threats against potential perpetrators, cautioning them that any sexual impropriety will bring

The House on Apple Blossom Lane

not just expulsion, but will be dealt with as harshly as the law will allow.

"I'm so sorry, Samantha. Is she okay?"

"No, not really. She has flashbacks all the time. And she's been in and out of rehab and counseling, and prescribed all sorts of antidepressants and antianxiety medications. She's even been hit with a couple mental illness diagnoses. PTSD and an anxiety disorder. That's why she lives at the house."

"What do you mean?"

"You don't know? Well, why would you, I guess. The house we're going to. Everyone that lives there is a trauma victim. Sorry, trauma *survivor*. They don't like the word *victim*."

"Wow, really?"

"You see that place across the street?," she turns and points at TRACE as they slow their ascent up the driveway to 6160. "It's part of the program that supports her here. They provide her with counseling and drugs and housing and even pay a part of her tuition. But even with all that she has a hard time paying for the rest of her bills, and can't hold down a job. So... she sells drugs sometimes. That's why Alice wants to see her. But the more she sells the more likely she is to get into trouble, and if she gets kicked out of school and loses the opportunity to become a mental health counselor helping others like her, which is the only prospect that seems to light her up anymore... If that happens, then I'm afraid that her future will be... dim."

"I see..." Duncan says, wondering where his dad fits in. Or if he even does. Suing the perpetrators of trauma? "This may seem like an odd question, but they don't have, like, a lawyer visit them for any reason, do they?"

"Not that I know of, why?"

'Shit!,' Duncan thinks. 'Why'd I ask her that? I should just tell her what I'm up to… no.' "I… When I got here I realized that I'd seen Apple Blossom Lane on a letter to my dad in his office once." 'Was that convincing?,' he wonders, staring into her bewitching eyes.

She says nothing for a second, narrowing those eyes, before saying: "Speaking of trauma, thank you for helping me out yesterday. I didn't get a chance to thank you at the time, I was… embarrassed."

"I'm happy I could help. What happened, anyway?"

She pauses again, not sure what to say.

"It's none of my business, sorry," Duncan says.

"You're sweet. No, it's okay. Let's just say he was being... presumptuous, and not acting like a gentleman."

"Fucking dick!," Duncan replies.

Samantha smiles and kisses him on the cheek. He feels like his breast may burst.

"My knight in shining armor," she says teasingly, leading him the final length of the driveway, opening the front door like she lives there. "I'm glad you're here, Ducan. I may need a hero to protect me from these horny college drunkards."

Chapter 3

The first thing that Duncan notices upon entering 6160 Apple Blossom Lane is that everything appears new. While the style of the home looks to match the others on the block, inside the home looks to have been recently constructed. It's an airy home with an open floorplan. Duncan follows Samantha through the foyer and to the right of the staircase, towards the sound of voices in the back. Coming into the kitchen, he meets the first two residents, who're talking to Michael and Alice.

His schoolmates are seated at the kitchen table beside another man and woman, both relatively young, yet noticeably older than their high school visitors; and not just in age, but in the stress they exhibit on their faces. Michael is leaning over the table with his face close to the other man's ear. The woman beside him is peppering the same man from the other side. Michael and the woman appear to be arguing against one another while attempting to keep their voices down, as if concerned that they'll be overheard. Everyone but Alice looks worried. As soon as they notice Duncan and Samantha approaching, they stop talking, staring at Duncan as if analyzing a threat.

"What?," Duncan asks.

No one speaks for a few seconds, then Samantha pipes up:

"What's the deal with you all? You're acting very strange today! It's just Duncan! Get over it!"

"This is my brother Dan," Michael says. Dan looks much the same as his younger brother, with the same cold, pale blue eyes, only more muscular and with some early signs of greying around his temples, as well as a small scar running a few inches above his left eyebrow.

"It's nice to meet you Dan," Duncan manages, fighting through the sense that he's anything but welcome. He steps forward and extends his hand. Dan shakes his hand firmly from his seated position, keeping his eyes earnestly locked onto Duncan's face the entire time, a quizzical, concerned look upon his countenance, as if performing a critical calculation. Michael wears a similar, albeit softer version of the same expression.

"And this is his girlfriend Mia," Michael adds. She's short and skinny, with straight, jet black hair and nervous mannerisms. But pleasant.

Mia smiles and shakes his hand. "Duncan," Duncan says.

"Don't worry about Daniel," Mia says. "He's wary of new people. He's been like that since the day that I met him. Like everyone's a potential hostile."

"Because everyone *is*," Dan interjects. "Some more likely so than others," he adds, staring lasers into Duncan's eyes. "Duncan, is it?" Duncan nods his head. "I don't mean to be rude, Duncan, but I don't think you should be here."

"Okay..." Duncan half-mumbles before turning to leave.

"What?," Samantha incredulously replies, putting her hands on Duncan's shoulders, holding him in place. "Are you serious Dan? Why on Earth would you say that? This better not be because of that stupid rumor about his father again!"

"No, I..." Dan looks away, then back. "I don't know anything about a *rumor*. It's just... he's too..." He searches for the words. "He's too... *young*," Dan presses, forcing the words out.

"Too young? We're all too 'young,'"
Samantha says, using air quotes to emphasize
the absurdity of the word *young*. "And we
come here almost every week."

"Yes," Dan replies, "but you guys are
different... you're family."

"Yea, well, Duncan here came to the rescue
of *this* particular family member yesterday,"
Samantha declares, "so he stays. Or I leave."

Dan stares at her as if reading a poker player,
then back and forth from her to Duncan, as if
seriously contemplating her proposition.

"Oh, let him stay Daniel," Mia says. "He's kind
of cute." She smiles. "In a befuddled, deer-in-
the-headlights kind of way. Look at him. He's
even lanky like a young buck."

"He's staying," Samantha commands. "And I'm going upstairs to see my sister. I assume she's here?"

"She's here," Mia confirms. Dan's eyes remain locked on Duncan, with Duncan doing his best not to notice, or show annoyance.

"You better not try to force him out while I'm gone," Samantha adds, moving Duncan to an open seat at the table and gently forcing him to sit in the chair. She turns to head towards the stairs.

"Did you bring a mask?," Dan asks, stopping her in her tracks.

"No, why, it's that bad? I thought it was safe to stop carrying them."

"I thought so too," Dan replies. "But apparently I was wrong. I just got back from dropping her off and then driving her back from the doctor's office an hour ago. She was too weak and out of it to drive herself. Apparently she has all the symptoms of COVID."

"But she's been vaccinated," Samantha states in confusion. "We both have."

"Yes, I know, we all have," Dan says. "And yet…"

"Thanks for driving her Dan. What symptoms does she have?," Samantha inquires with clear concern.

"She's been coughing hard on and off since yesterday, almost wheezing at times, and complaining of a sore throat and trouble breathing. And she barely had the energy to get up and go to her appointment. The doctor drew blood for testing. We're worried she might have to be hospitalized if things get any worse. We're all afraid to even get close to her. We deal with enough, as you know. I don't know how she's going to keep up with school, honestly. Hopefully she'll be able to get an extension on most of her work."

"It was just a mild cough, a headache and a slight temperature when I talked to her a couple of days ago," Samantha notes. "The flu? It is flu season…"

"Maybe," Dan says doubtfully.

Loud coughing is heard upstairs, in the back of the house. Samantha starts to run for the stairs.

"Wait! Here, take a mask. Luckily we still have some around." Dan retrieves a mask from a drawer near the kitchen sink and hands it to Samantha, who dons it on her way upstairs.

A few seconds later, they hear Samantha knock, and an argument ensue, their voices growing ever louder, then falling off. Soon thereafter, Samantha comes back down the stairs, looking frightened and deflated.

"She won't let me in," she complains. "She's worried that she'll get me sick."

"She's probably right," Michael flatly states. "We don't need the flu running amuck at the high school, do we? Or whatever it is…"

"Real compassionate, Mike!," Samantha seethes.

"What? I'm just saying…"

Nothing is said for a few seconds, then Alice breaks the silence. "You mind if I take a hit, Dan?," she asks, motioning with her head towards the pipe and baggie of marijuana buds on the kitchen counter.

"Go for it," Dan replies. Alice reaches into the baggie and breaks apart a nug, placing the pieces in the bowl of the pipe. Mia gets up to join her.

"I still don't understand how you guys can smoke so much of that shit in this house," Samantha states, sounding perturbed. "Doesn't it, like, mix badly with the meds that they give you."

"Believe it or not it's one of the few things that really helps," Dan says. "I think I'd be on a lot more medication without it. Or drinking a lot more. Pick your poison. As poisons go, marijuana barely qualifies, if at all."

"Whatever," Samantha irritably exclaims, looking up at the ceiling towards her sister's room. They hear another coughing spell. Mia retrieves a few beers from the fridge. She opens and hands one to Samantha.

"There's nothing that you can do right now," she says to Samantha, placing a hand on her shoulder and attempting to console her. "Just try to relax. Let's... show your cute new friend here how we roll. Besides, it looks like he's even more in need of a drink than you!"

Samantha turns and smiles at Duncan while Mia hands him a beer, adding a smile of her own. He's unused to the female attention, his blood pressure spiking. It's like his heart is doing cartwheels.

"Awwww... look how cute he looks when he gets nervous," Mia says. "Samantha, look at him! His face is turning red," she teases. "It matches his hair!"

Taking a chug of her beer, Samantha smiles again, broader than before.

"To new friends," Mia says, holding her bottle out for a cheers. They clink their three bottles together, and Duncan takes a chug, trying not to cough at the taste. He's only been intoxicated once in his life, a couple days after his mother died, stealing a fifth of vodka from his parents' liquor cabinet and guzzling it while walking around their upscale neighborhood. But these are very different circumstances. Finally, he's spending time with the girl of his dreams. And even though there's something strange about this place, and that it's more than a little disconcerting that his father's office directed him here, he's wanted absolutely *anything* to do with Samantha for so long that he feels giddy. Within minutes everyone is drinking, and a few friends of Mia's arrive, followed shortly thereafter by the other two residents of the house, George and Greta. George yells "TGIF!" as he walks through the door. "Mia, beer me!," he adds.

George and Greta look similar, as if they're siblings. 'Perhaps they are,' Duncan thinks. Both have blonde hair and look Northern European. Swedish or Norwegian, perhaps. Maybe Danish. George, however, is short and rotund, whereas Greta is a svelte little rail of a young woman, and looks athletic. Maybe a gymnast. They enter the residence as if attached at the hip. 'Siblings, or a couple,' he thinks as they enter the fray, Greta somewhat reluctantly.

Alice drinks and smokes more than anyone, and before long her rate of intoxication triggers Michael who, seemingly not for the first time, is cautioning her to slow down. As a couple more guys arrive holding six packs, Mia starts back in on Duncan, who's still glued to his seat. He's afraid to move for fear of waking and spoiling the ideal dream of having Samantha Conway keen on him, even as everyone else moves around him, their movement accelerating with the intoxication.

"He's a lightweight!," Mia declares to Samantha as Duncan shyly sips at his bottle of beer. She whispers something in Samantha's ear. As Samantha takes her first hit from the pipe, Mia asks Duncan:

"You heard of shotgunning a hit, Duncan?"

"No, I haven't. I've only been high a couple of times..." he lies. He's only smoked once. And he was so afraid of it that he didn't really inhale.

"Don't worry, you'll like it, I promise." Samantha finishes taking a long draw from the pipe, holding it in, then walks towards Duncan.

"Open your mouth, cutie, and prepare to inhale!" Mia commands.

Duncan complies and, as he does so, Samantha bends down and presses her mouth to his, exhaling the smoke slowly from her lungs while kissing Duncan, softly at first, then with relish. He's so overcome with exuberance from his first kiss with Samantha that he almost forgets that he just inhaled smoke, only recalling upon feeling the burning sensation in his throat and lungs. He starts to exhale, but it's too late, and

Samantha pulls away as he coughs with sudden violence, his whole body shaking.

Samantha laughs and pats him on the back. His head spins, from the marijuana or the kiss, he can't be sure. Likely from the combination of the two. She sits on his lap and smiles at him. Grabbing and taking a swig from his bottle, she goes in for another kiss, passing some of the beer to him in the process. It's the greatest thrill of his life. So overcome with emotion is he that he barely notices the odd odor permeating the air. 'Maybe it's the marijuana,' he thinks, before someone else notices it.

"Do you guys smell that?," one of Mia's friends asks.

Everyone stops and takes a whiff. It smells strange. Like a mixture of Sulphur and burning rubber.

"Yea," George says. "Something smells funny. What *is* that?"

"Good question," Dan says. "Maybe there's something wrong with the heater."

"But didn't they, like, just rebuild the entire house?," Mia asks. "The heater is new, isn't it?"

"I think so," Dan says. He stares at Duncan, but Duncan doesn't notice. Neither does Samantha. They're far too focused on one another, trading soft kisses, Samantha still on his lap, nibbling at him teasingly across the table from Dan. Dan gets up and ambles uneasily out the back door, favoring his left leg. Duncan looks up right as Dan slides the glass door closed, just catching a glimpse of Dan's eyes. They're fierce and focused, and the eye contact has a brief, sobering effect on Duncan, making him pay more attention.

Duncan watches as Dan takes his cell phone from his pocket, dials a number and then presses the phone to his ear. He walks away from the house and off to the right, towards the granny unit situated in the back right portion of the property. Duncan leans in his chair to follow him with his eyes, but Dan drifts out of sight.

"What is it?," Samantha asks, sensing his change in demeanor.

"I don't know," he says. "Probably nothing."

"Don't worry about Dan, he's been through a lot," she says, trying to assuage his concern. "His mood can swing suddenly and he has a hard time sitting still. And it takes him a long time to get comfortable with new people. Trust me, I know. It took him months to accept my visits; even longer before I felt truly accepted by him. And I think he only came around because he likes my sister."

"Why? Why is he like that?"

"Afghanistan," Samantha responds. "I don't know the whole story. Something about his company being ambushed in what they thought was a friendly village. He barely made it out. Mia told me once that he didn't *really* make it out. That his mind is still there. To this day he can't see someone reach into their pockets without being set on edge and reflexively reaching for a phantom gun on a combat belt that he isn't even wearing. Which is why this program he's in is such a godsend for him..."

"The TRAC people? Or TRACE?," Duncan inquires.

"Yea. The thing I was telling you about outside. Trauma Research and Counseling. They have a whole program on campus; their own curriculum. And their extension across the street makes treating these residents easier. It provides more direct access. My sister raves about it. Says she wouldn't be able to handle things without it. They help everyone here with their expenses, and provide counseling and meds... it's amazing."

"A nonprofit?"

"I think so," Samantha replies. "PR for Big Pharma, I think. You know, so we don't think them heartless moneygrubbers. And Dan timed it perfectly, apparently. In fact, right after he was accepted into the program TRAC decided that this house needed a makeover. They redid everything... new appliances, floor, countertops, and added the extra unit in the back of the property. They're well-funded, I guess. Big Pharma makes a ton of money, of course."

"My mom worked for a pharmaceutical company," Duncan says. He's about to open up about his mother's death when, peering out the back door, Dan momentarily comes back into view from the right. He has his back to him as he enters Duncan's field of vision, but quickly turns his head around, as if feeling Duncan's eyes on him. Their eyes meet, with Dan's eyes holding the same intensity in them as before. There's something deeply suspicious and threatening about them. Dan turns and walks back to the right out of sight just as the front door opens, and someone else enters the home.

"Sir Charles!," Greta yells. She hops down from the counter where she'd been sitting sipping on her beer and runs at the man. He looks a little too old to be a college student, with a goatee, curly brown hair and clever eyes, which go to work assessing the scene. They look from one person to the next, then to the substances on the counter. He seems more attuned to the situation than the others.

As soon as his eyes fall on Duncan he stops, then cocks his head to the side, like a dog does when it's attempting comprehension.

"Who are *you*?," he asks, seemingly more out of concern than curiosity. "I don't know you…"

"Oh, for Chrissakes!," Samantha half shouts, getting up off Duncan's lap. "What is the deal with everyone?" As loud as she can manage, over the trance music someone has started in the living room, she announces: "Everyone, this is Duncan! He's my friend from the high school! He's harmless! Lay down your damn arms! Duncan, this is Charlie. They call him Sir Charles for some reason."

Charlie chuckles, then says: "Well, if you're Sam's friend, you're good enough for me." Duncan isn't convinced.

"Too good!," Greta giggles, embracing Charlie firmly. "Sir Charles works across the street, and sneaks over here sometimes," she adds.

"Yes, but don't tell my boss," he grins. "So," he continues, "how is everyone feeling this evening?"

"Pretty damn good, sir!," Greta says with another laugh. 'Yea, pretty damn good,' Duncan thinks.

"Do you smell anything, Charlie?," Mia asks.

Charlie takes a long whiff of the air, then: "Just marijuana, but that's nothing new around here."

"You know what, I don't smell it anymore either," Mia realizes.

"Smell what?," Charlie asks. "What did it smell like...?"

They all look at one another, trying to find the words to describe the alien scent, but they can't decide on an accurate description.

"Well, I doubt it's important," Charlie judges. Everyone nods in agreement, even Duncan, though in the back of his mind he isn't so sure. It certainly was a strong smell, and very strange…

"So," Charlie chimes back in, "y'all know how much I love to play games, and I just learned a new one. I thought that we could give it a try. What do y'all say?"

Some nod in agreement, many say "yes." Duncan himself finds it a surprisingly good idea, suddenly feeling eager to try a new game. Everyone, in fact, seems to love the idea, and excitement ensues.

Charlie walks over to the fridge and grabs an armful of beers, then invites them all into the living room on the left side of the house. They gather around the large coffee table, some sitting on the couches, others on the ground. Charlie turns the volume down on the stereo, then pulls a pack of cards from his pocket. As

 The House on Apple Blossom Lane

he starts to shuffle them Dan comes back into the house, scowling noticeably upon seeing Charlie. Charlie nods his head at him, a stoic expression upon his face. Dan forces a return nod, and instead of joining the others around the coffee table, leans against the wall near the entryway.

"The game is called 'Drink or Dare,'" Charlie announces. "This is how it works: I pass out cards, including one to myself, and we go in order of card rank, from the Ace of Spades on down, with the one with the highest card going first. The cardholder dares whomever they want to do something, and that person either does it, or drinks a beer. Then we determine who's next, and they do the same, choosing someone to dare, and on, until everyone's had a turn."

'My God, I'm way too shy for this game,' Duncan thinks. 'I guess I'm just going to have to get drunk...'

Charlie passes out the cards, then asks: "So, does anyone have an ace?"

No one answers, then he says: "I do, actually. So I'll demonstrate by making a dare that I *know* will lead to a drink, to get things started."

Charlie peers around at the other players, before settling his eyes on Alice, who's more intoxicated than the rest of the group, being partially held in the upright position by Michael. "Alice, I dare you to…" He looks around the table. "…to make out with George."

Michael scoffs, then says: "Don't be absurd Charlie, there's no way that she's going to…"

Then, to everyone's surprise, Alice gets up and begins walking over to the other side of the table, where George is seated next to Greta. Michael tries to hold her back, gently at first. "Stop messing around Alice… what the hell..." but she fights him off, and he lets her go. "Fine, okay, whatever Alice, go ahead and..." he sounds disbelieving, as though he's calling her bluff, but she kneels down next to big George and tries to kiss him.

It appears to upset Greta at first, and George resists, but Charlie says "It's okay, Greta, it's just a kiss. Go ahead and kiss her George." Then Greta leans away, and George begins to reciprocate the kiss with Alice. Michael, standing halfway between where he was seated and where his girlfriend is making out with another guy, fumes silently. Everyone is shocked, putting their hands to their mouths or gawking in disbelief. Samantha lets out a little snicker, receiving a menacing glare from Michael in response. Charlie is the only one who doesn't seem surprised. Alice and George keep kissing, Greta looking at them as if in shock, but not intervening. "Does anyone have a king?," Charles asks.

"I do," Michael replies from his standing position, keeping his eyes locked on Samantha. "Sam, I dare you to go give your sister a big hug."

"But," Samantha protests while standing, "she already said she won't see me. Why would she..."

"Tell her it's important," Michael continues, "that you need to see her. *Make* her let you in."

"Michael, what the fuck?," Duncan protests.

"Shut up, Duncan! You shouldn't even be here!," he retorts.

But Samantha barely even hesitates. She's headed towards the staircase, despite protestations from Duncan and not wearing a mask, and with Dan yelling behind her: "It's a bad idea, Sam, she's really sick!" He moves to intervene, as if to forcefully stop her from climbing the stairs, but then Charlie says:

"Let her go, Dan. No cheating! No interfering in the game!" Dan locks in place, then rocks back and forth, as if teetering with equivocation. "A queen, anyone?," Charlie asks.

"Me," Greta says. "Dan, come over here and pull Alice off of George. I can't bring myself to do it..." Her eyes are tearing up as she watches Alice and George slobbering all over one another, as if no one else is around. Dan, already angry, crosses the room quickly and pulls Alice off of George, who tries to pull her back. "Stop him!," Greta shouts. This starts a wrestling match between Dan and George, which quickly begins to escalate, Dan shoving George into the wall, causing a picture to fall off and a vase to fall from a table and shatter. Charlie giggles, then covers his mouth.

Duncan gets up and, suddenly fearing for Samantha, runs up the stairs and to the back of the house. He sees the door wide open, and Samantha and her sister embracing just outside her door, despite the fact that her sister, Caroline, shows definite signs of distress. Her face is red and she's sweating. She starts to cough. Samantha turns and sees him, then yells: "Go away Duncan, I don't want you getting sick!"

Duncan runs back down the stairs, completely discombobulated. "What the hell is going on?," he asks aloud to no one in particular. Looking in on the game, he sees that the other two guys, Mia's friends, have started undressing her, and that Dan and George are at one another's throats, now quite literally. Duncan locks eyes with Charlie, and has a hard time comprehending the emotion that they're conveying. His hand is over his mouth, but it looks like he's smiling. A second later and his eyes are on Duncan. The grin drops

     The House on Apple Blossom Lane

away from his face. His eyes are cold. Lifeless and piercing.

"Strip down and run home," Charlie orders him.

'That's ridiculous,' Duncan thinks. But suddenly he's doing it. Shirt, then belt, then pants, then underwear, socks and shoes, and he's out the door.

It's raining lightly. It's cold, but it doesn't seem to matter. All he can think about is home. His father and his girlfriend. 'I have to run home to Dad and Marie.'

He starts running, past his car, his manhood flailing in the refracted glare of the overcast afternoon. He makes it a few blocks before he really starts sucking in the air, then suddenly feels dizzy. His fingers and toes start to tingle. He slows his run into a jog, then a walk, then stops. He stands there for a minute before thinking: 'What the hell am I doing?' He sits down on the curb, then realizes that a couple of girls holding books are watching him, giggling. He's near the driveway into the college, College Way. He turns around, walking back towards his car and the house, his head spinning.

When he reaches his car he sees Charlie exiting the house. Duncan stops next to his car to watch him. "Stop doing what you're doing," Charlie yells back into the house through the doorway before walking out and closing the door, a queer little smile on his face. He puts the pack of cards back in their case and into his pants pocket before pulling his cell phone from the other pocket. He types something briefly into his phone, then walks down the driveway to the street. That's when he turns and sees Duncan standing next to his car, naked. He shakes his head.

"What the hell is wrong with you kid?," he asks. "Put on some clothes and go home." Duncan says nothing, just stares at him, an odd sense of shifting reality battling in his brain. Charlie crosses the street, gets in a black Toyota Forerunner parked in front of TRACE and then gives Duncan one last long look before driving away.

Duncan takes a few deep breaths, feeling a sense of sobriety slowly reenter his being with each breath. After a minute of this he walks back into the house. The first thing he notices upon entering is another odd smell, though this one different than before. This odor is more like a mix of something minty with something sour. Mia is getting dressed. Her two friends sit next to her with their hands on their heads. Greta is shaking George, trying to revive him; he appears unconscious. Dan is wiping blood from his nose. Alice and Michael are in a corner, arguing with one another. Upstairs Duncan hears Samantha chatting with her sister Caroline. Duncan thinks he hears Caroline say: "I shouldn't have let you in. What the hell was I thinking. I don't see how this can be COVID though…"

Duncan retrieves his clothes from the bottom of the stairs and gets dressed quickly. He thinks of going upstairs and talking to Samantha, and trying to help, unable to believe the turn that things have taken. He went from having the time of his life to *The Twilight Zone*. But he can't bring himself to climb the stairs. "It's my boyfriend," he hears Greta say from the kitchen. "He's been knocked out, but I don't know how."

Duncan exits the house, gets in his car and starts the drive home, passing a police car a few blocks away, its sirens blaring as it shoots back towards 6160. Suddenly, a massive headache and state of confusion overcomes him, and he pulls over to the side of the road.

'I know that police car has something to do with me, but I don't know what…' he thinks. 'What have I been doing all afternoon? I went down this lane to find my father, but did I...? Was I drinking?'

Terror grips him as he realizes that he's lost track of time, and as he drives home he attempts in vain to retrace his steps, feeling as if, somewhere along the path, those steps led him into a black hole.

Chapter 4

Try as he might, Duncan can't clearly materialize yesterday in his mind. It's not that it's entirely blank, but more of an incoherent haze; like an interweave of fact and fantasy that he's unable to disentangle. What did he imagine? What did he dream? What actually happened? And it's not just the memory that's obscure.

His emotional connection to yesterday is mixed up, as if neither his heart nor mind can decipher what occurred, or how to feel about it. There are feelings of elation countered by feelings of dread and terror, like having found his way into a calm, welcoming bay only to be subsequently imperiled by a savage storm.

Samantha! 'I remember kissing her, but I honestly can't say for sure that it happened while I was awake. The last thing that I clearly recall was deciding to find out what my father really does… imagining that he was consigliere to some mafia don or something. That guy that picked him up, a sheer block of Italian marble, he was. And… Grace! Dad's secretary. She gave me the address on Apple Blossom Lane, and I got there but… what..? It was a college community, next to the healthcare college… and an address that kept recurring in my head… 6160!'

Duncan lurches out of bed, feeling as though he has an anvil tied around his neck, and stumbles over to his laptop. Typing 6160 Apple Blossom Lane into Google Maps, he immediately notices that it's directly across from a place called TRACE, which rings a bell. Clicking on the acronym, he's back on the Trauma Research and Counseling Extension page of the Pacific Northwest Healthcare College website, leading him back to TRAC: "On TRAC: Giving back to the community since 2013." 'Yes! This is familiar! I looked this up yesterday.'

Again he reads: "The mission of The TRAC Foundation is to provide financial, academic and psychological support for trauma survivors nationwide. We offer housing, counseling and funding for trauma victims aspiring to earn their degrees, as well as program assistance for universities dedicated to better understanding and treating trauma." The bell of recollection rings a little louder. 'Something about Samantha's sister, and Michael's brother… Dan! Yes, Dan!' He sees snapshots in his mind of Dan eyeing him suspiciously while on the phone in the backyard, followed by a swelling of heart recalling Samantha seated on his lap, blowing marijuana smoke into his mouth. 'It must have been some super potent stuff,' he thinks. 'Or maybe there was something else in the pipe..?' He looks at the computer screen again, and the list of "Our Sponsors" near the top.

There are four pharmaceutical companies listed, followed by defense contractor Haliburton, The Veterans Administration and Washington State. 'Wait a second,' he thinks, focusing in on one of the pharmaceutical sponsors, 'that's Mom's company! How did I not notice that yesterday?' BridleChem, where his mother Darla worked as a research and development chemist, is listed third out of the four representatives of Big Pharma.

Immediately memories begin flooding into his mind. His mother returning from work, always stressed, always arguing with his father about something. The fights never lasted long, however. And my God, did they love each other! But she wasn't happy. She wanted to quit, in fact. Something about the job that she "couldn't stomach anymore." But Dad convinced her to stay somehow, for some reason. "Let's talk about it after Mexico," he'd told her. *Mexico*. The vacation that changed everything. He recalls what his father told his brother, sister and him just before they buried her.

"Your mother came from a well-off family, as you all know. And the cartels in Mexico track these things. In fact, one of their primary sources of income is to abduct and hold members of wealthy families for ransom. Your mom and I knew this, but we were assured by the authorities that Puerto Vallarta was safe; that the cartels didn't venture into popular tourist destinations. Apparently they made an exception... maybe they were hard up for cash or something, there's no way to know for sure. Anyway... a few gunmen came into our resort and grabbed her, and there just happened to be an undercover cop on duty, and there was a firefight... it happened so fast, and an errant shot hit your mom."

On an impulse he types "Darla Mills Puerto Vallarta" into Google. The first result is a newspaper report out of Mexico City from around the time of her death with her name and the name of her company, BridleChem, in it. Copying and pasting the story into a translator site, he reads: "Darla Mills, Chief R&D Chemist for Washington-State-based BridleChem Pharmaceuticals, and Forest Honeycutt, BridleChem Chief Counsel, gunned down in botched cartel kidnapping, say authorities. But is that what really happened?"

Duncan's eyes bounce from spot to spot in the article, his blood pressure escalating with each jump. "...suspicious circumstances... witnesses state that Mills and Honeycutt were meeting with suspected members of the Tijuana Cartel at Taqueria Santa Rita in Ameca."

'Fuck! Dad lied! It didn't happen in some posh resort in some protected tourist haven! I've never even heard of Ameca.' Looking it up, he finds that Ameca is 135 miles from Puerto

Vallarta; several hours by car, and closer to Guadalajara than Puerto Vallarta.

He reads on: "Investigators suspect that members of the Sinaloa Cartel broke up the meeting between the BridleChem employees and the Tijuana Cartel members with a hail of machine gun bullets... eight dead, one critically wounded... survivor Tito Encenillo transported to local hospital... expected to survive his wounds... told this reporter that the purpose of the meeting was to negotiate the terms of a cartel merger masterminded by the head of a narcotics syndicate named Señor Arbusto."

Reading on: "When pressed by our investigator to identify this so-called mastermind, Mr. Encenillo said: "I don't know who he is. All I can say for sure is that they're rumors that he used to run the country, and that he inherited both that position and this subsequent narco-king crown from his father. They say he mostly just mooches off of his name and his dead daddy's legacy and connections. They say all his dad's shady business interests provided the operation's infrastructure; all the political and law enforcement protections and purchased loyalties and laundering fronts. They say the whole operation is based upon his dad's connection to the intelligence community, and his knowledge of narcotics financing military operations in the late 20th century.""

Duncan continues reading, finding near the end of the article: "While at first refusing to comment, BridleChem spokeswoman Mary McConnell recently reached out to our investigative reporter, Emilio Sanchez, to make the following statement: "While their act was not officially sanctioned by BridleChem, Darla and Forest were both tireless advocates for the underprivileged, and had long spoken of funding healthcare clinics in the most impoverished regions of Mexico and other underdeveloped nations ravaged by violence and disease, even if it meant spending their own hard-earned money. We can only surmise that they were compelled to seek permission from the cartels controlling the lawless regions of that nation most in need of such assistance, and paid for it with their lives."''

'I knew she had predilections towards philanthropy, but I don't recall either her or Dad talking about anything like that.' He looks back over the article. The name of the single survivor of the shooting, "Tito Encenillo," is a blue underlined link. Duncan clicks on it, quickly learning: "Tito Encenillo, suspected Tijuana Cartel soldier, was killed in Pistalone Prison yesterday just prior to his arraignment for multiple counts of homicide and narcotics trafficking. Stabbed sixteen times with an unknown weapon, likely a prison shiv...The killing appears to be gang related. Authorities have been unable to produce any witnesses. Detective Juan Gonzalez reports that: "It's yet another unfortunate incidence of powerful entities operating with near impunity within

Mexico possessing far more resources than law enforcement can effectively counter.'"

'Jesus Christ!,' Duncan thinks. Clicking back to the original article, he follows links to his mom, to Forest Honeycutt, and to BridleChem. He reads his mother's biography, including of her philanthropic efforts with underprivileged youth and her love of nature. Most of it he's familiar with, until Mexico is mentioned again at the bottom of her "In Memoria" page: "In honor of Darla Mills, the generous BridleChem chemist who lost her life trying to pave the way to a better life for Mexico's most needy citizens, BridleChem is dedicating a million dollars a year to the establishment and ongoing operation of healthcare clinics throughout Mexico's rural regions, to be administered by our partner Trauma Research and Counseling. The clinics will provide highly needed medicines as well as mental health counseling for the countless victims of narcoviolence."

'Why hasn't Dad mentioned this?,' he wonders. He then reads of Forest Honeycutt; of his brief background as a lobbyist "on Capitol Hill," and his five years serving as an aide to Supreme Court Chief Justice Roberts before "heading west to help establish BridleChem." And then he reads of BridleChem itself. A young company founded in 2010, just a few years before TRAC, its Board of Directors is comprised of a cadre of East Coast big wigs. Sprinkled amongst the investment bankers and hedge fund managers are a former DC District Attorney, two former senators and the former Director of the FBI, all "proudly supporting the vision of Christian Carpenter."

'Christian Carpenter. Could that be Mr. C., Dad's boss?' Duncan clicks on Christian Carpenter, underlined and in blue, taking him to the top of the "TRAC Chief Officers" page. "Christian Carpenter, CEO." Duncan stares at his picture on the page, knowing immediately that he's seen him before. 'He's been here at the house a bunch of times. He's the one with the super-hot blonde wife that's always staring absent-mindedly out the window with a far-off, melancholy look on her face, like she might break down and start crying at any minute. I remember thinking how much of a shame it was that such a beautiful woman could look so miserable.'

Refocusing his gaze on Carpenter, Carpenter's eyes seem to reach out and lock onto him, like a tractor beam pulling him inexorably towards an abyss. His hair is dark and short, a military cut speckled with grey. He has a slight cleft on his chin, a prominent nose with a bump in the center and bronze skin. Likely of Mediterranean descent. He might almost be handsome, if it wasn't for those eyes. They're sunken, as though retreating into his face, wary of seeing anything more. And they're dark, like his hair, but darker, and not just in color. He's smiling broadly in the polished picture, but it doesn't matter. His eyes are anything *but* smiling. They're deep and deathly, undercutting the smile. It's as though they're coals plucked from the bowels of Hell, ripped from the face of a demon and stuffed into the skull of one incapable of joy.

Duncan has a hard time pulling his eyes from those of Carpenter's visage in order to read his bio: "Third generation Italian-American, Christian Carpenter hails from a proud American military family. His grandfather served honorably during World War Two. A sniper with twenty-two confirmed kills under his belt that helped the Allies reclaim his homeland, "He would've killed Mussolini himself if the partisans hadn't gotten to him first," Christian proudly reports. "Christian's father was an intelligence officer for the Army during both the Korean and Vietnam Wars, helping expose the plots of dictators and communists and to emancipate the citizens of those countries from both evils before helping to install freedom and democracy in their place."

 The House on Apple Blossom Lane

Duncan reads on: "My father instilled the wisdom deep within me that every warrior's foremost weapon is his mind. Those that're too quick to pull their sword from its sheath demonstrate the fact that their deadliest weapon has gone dull, and that they've become their own enemy. Of course, it's another thing entirely when that foremost weapon is cracked or broken, as I know firsthand. I'll do whatever it takes to help those that make it out of their own brushes with death, and help them reforge the swords with which they fight evil."

"As a captain in the War For a Free Iraq, Christian and his squad were evacuating Iraqi civilians from an apartment tower in the city of Kirkuk in Northern Iraq in 2010 when an IED toppled the building, trapping Christian and the surviving members of his squad inside. For four days and three nights Christian and the six members of the squad that survived the collapse defended themselves against countless enemies, enduring ordinance of every order, before reinforcements finally rescued them on the fourth day. Only Christian and two other members of his squad were pulled from the wreckage, all three of them badly wounded. The other two surviving members of his platoon, Ron Jenkins and Gerald O'Keefe, both privates, attested to Christian's bravery, vowing that they owed their lives to their leader's unparalleled valor. While recovering from his wounds, Christian was awarded the Army Distinguished Service Cross, promoted to colonel and recruited to join the Military Intelligence Corps. But his *mental wounds* lingered."

"I did my best to carry on," Christian reports, "but eventually I had to concede the fact that a warrior without his mind is no warrior at all. And when I returned to The States, I learned more and more the disheartening lesson of how many soldiers live with such taxing, deeply-ingrained, debilitating trauma; trauma that holds them captive, keeping them from recovering themselves and living their lives. I was determined. I realized that *this* is my war, and I fought furiously to recruit a new kind of army; an army of compassion."

"Working with the woefully underfunded Veterans Administration as the conflicts in the Middle East were winding down under President Obama, Christian quickly made powerful allies in government at the state and federal levels whom thereafter connected him to prominent professionals in the psychiatric and pharmaceutical industries. Moved by his impassioned quest, Christian's army grew, and in 2013 TRAC was born in the Pacific Northwest, equipped to help veterans recover lives lost to trauma. Soon, he found that trauma is tragically common in society, and began offering assistance to *all* PTSD sufferers, regardless of cause."

'If this *is* who my father works for, it certainly *sounds* like a worthwhile endeavor,' Duncan thinks. 'Why, then, does Michael, and maybe his brother and everyone else, think that my father's a crook and works for someone dangerous? And what is this cartel connection? And these lies about my mother? I mean, *someone* is lying. My Dad or her former company or this... Mexico City Times.' Duncan feels his headache worsen, and tries to take some deep breaths, but between his poor recall of the day before and all this confusing, conflicting information, the attempt falters. 'I don't care if it pisses him off, or scares Marie, he's going to tell me the truth!'

But by the time Duncan reaches the kitchen table, he's lost his determination, capitulating to the doubt, the pounding headache and two days of worry and poor sleep. 'Who am I to make demands of my father?,' he thinks. Yet Jonathan Mills is acting off, and so is Marie. They both look haggard, like they're more sleep deprived and under even more duress than he is. They keep looking at him, stealing furtive, anxious glances, then looking away, like they want to talk to him but don't know what to say. And there's a tiny bottle of some clear solution on the counter. 'Sanitizer?' Duncan wonders. 'He's never used it before, not even when the COVID thing was in full-blown public-panicking epidemic mode.'

Duncan gobbles down his breakfast as though he hasn't eaten in a week, but neither his father nor Marie can do more than push their food around on their plates whilst eyeing him. 'What's their deal?,' he wonders. 'I expected that *I'd* be the oddity at the table, not them.' Marie reaches across the table and grasps Jonathan's hand, squeezing it gently in a show of support. Finally Jonathan breaks through his own trepidation and speaks up:

"Did you go straight to school yesterday, like I told you to, Duncan?"

"Y... yes, yes sir. Why do you ask?"

His father lets out a deep, shaking sigh, as if trying not to explode.

"You wouldn't lie to me, now, *would you,* Duncan?"

Duncan just looks at him, saying nothing.

"Your father is just trying to protect you sweetie, because he loves you, you know that, right?," Marie assures him.

"Protect me from what, exactly?"

Jonathan and Marie look at one another, searching for the words.

"I tried to tell you yesterday, Duncan. There are certain... *forces* in this world that nothing can perfectly... contain. You've lived a very safe, comfortable life, son, and that tends to make people... *complacent*. It tends to give them a false sense of security. We have everything we need, yes. And the protection of the law, yes. But you have to understand that money, law, my abilities... they all have limits. And there are some things, some people and powers... that operate *beyond* those limits. There are some things that you don't want to know. And I don't want you to find them out the hard way, okay?"

Duncan stares into his father's dark brown eyes for a few seconds, then some combination of anger and courage take hold of him, and he responds:

"You mean like Mom did?"

Marie gasps softly, seemingly shocked, whereas his father comes as close to enraged as he's ever seen him. Jonathan reaches across the table and grasps his son by the upper arm, squeezing ferociously.

"What the hell did you just say? Why would you say that? Tell me right now, Duncan, or I swear to God I'll..."

"I looked it up, okay?," Duncan replies. His father loosens his grip. "I was thinking about Mom yesterday and I looked her up, *that's* why I say that!," he lies. "What's wrong with that?"

Jonathan releases his grip, and after a few seconds of silence, answers: "There's nothing wrong with that, son. Nothing." He pauses again, then says: "But I told you what happened to her."

"You didn't tell us the truth Dad, did you? You told us... what was it? That a cartel tried to kidnap her in a resort in Puerta Vallarta on your vacation! That's what you told us! But that's not what the Mexican newspapers said! It didn't even *happen* in Puerto Vallarta! It was in some little town! And they say that she was *meeting* with the cartel! That she was involved with them somehow! They implied that she was doing business with them! They practically said she was a member! Like she deserved it!"

"She didn't deserve to die, Duncan, you need to know that."

"Okay... Then why lie about it, Dad?"

"Because... because there were a lot of ugly, wild rumors circulating about it back then, and I didn't want to upset you kids more than you already were. There was even an FBI investigation into your mother, but they dropped it when..." his voice falters, and he looks away... "when they realized that they didn't have a case." He looks back at Duncan, then away again, adding: "She was doing philanthropy."

"You said you two were on vacation, Dad!"

"So I lied about it being a vacation. It wasn't. Not entirely. As for *why* I lied, why *we* lied before we left, we did it because we didn't want you or your brother or sister to worry. And I lied when I got back because I didn't want you to get hurt by the stories, or to be mad at me for not protecting her. I was hating myself so much... for letting that happen to her. I think that I couldn't bear the idea of you kids hating me too." Marie reaches over and gives his hand another squeeze. "But the truth is I *knew* it was dangerous. I'd just started representing a partner of your mom's company, and I found out about... some projects they were considering, and I insisted on going, but... I wasn't allowed to go to that meeting. Believe me, I tried. They didn't trust me yet, I guess. But it might've been for the best, because *if* I'd gone you guys might've buried us both."

It's silent around the table for a few seconds, then Duncan meekly asks:

"She was meeting with a Mexican drug cartel? *Really?*"

     The House on Apple Blossom Lane

"That country is fucked up, Duncan. There are places in the world where you need to buy the permission of the bad guys in order to help those in need and be one of the good guys. There are a lot of fucked up things out there Duncan, like I've been trying to tell you. Excuse my French. And speaking of... f'd up, I need you to take this."

He opens the cap and turns the bottle of clear liquid over into Duncan's glass of orange juice, adding: "I think that I may've been exposed to something at work. This is like the... vaccine, just in case I've exposed you. Marie already took hers."

"Exposed to what?," Duncan asks.

"Apparently it's a mutated strain of COVID. Something that the COVID-9 vaccine doesn't protect against."

This rings a bell in the back of Duncan's mind, but he can't place it. Duncan gulps down his orange juice before asking: "And how in the hell were you exposed to it?"

"One of my clients works for a drug development company. They were trying to understand how the virus might mutate on its own, so they could try to get out ahead of it and develop new vaccines before it hits. So they... *manipulated* it. They're afraid it might've gotten out. It's this whole big thing. Major potential lawsuits and labor law violations, and extreme stress and hours of extra work for me."

'That must be why the two of them look so worn out,' Duncan thinks.

"You have to promise me, Duncan, that you'll stop this thing about my work... just ask me if you have questions. You go poking around hornet's nests and you're liable to get stung, and some hornets have bigger stingers than others. And when the whole nest is cracked and they start to swarm..." He stops, as if unable to finish the thought, it's so horrible. "Just ask me instead, so you can avoid it. I've been inside many of those nests. You don't want to follow me, please trust me on that, okay?"

"What *nests*, Dad?"

Jonathan Mills pauses, searching his son's eyes. "Let's just say that I'm not in love with everyone that I represent, but it's my job, okay?"

While the day before is still a blur, Duncan feels much better by the time he makes it back up to his room. He's finally taking full breaths, having restored his faith in his father. But the preceding day's events are still maddeningly misplaced. He's getting snapshots. He thinks he was in the house that Grace gave him the address for, but as for what transpired there... it's like some of it won't surface, and the stuff that does, he can't be sure if he experienced or imagined it.

He badly wants to talk to Samantha, or at least to Michael and Alice, and try to sort through what happened, but he doesn't have any of their numbers. So he resolves to approach them when school resumes on Monday, hoping that the haze will clear on its own.

'In the meantime, I'll just fantasize about being Samantha's boyfriend, and making all the jocks jealous when we walk by them every day, hand in hand.'

Chapter 5

While the attempt to generate some clarity on the events of Friday afternoon persist throughout the weekend, Duncan remains unable to distinguish what actually happened from what he may well have imagined. Worse, he's unable to admit the struggle to his father or to Marie, as it would entail admitting that he disobeyed his father's order and then lied to him about going to the house on Apple Blossom Lane. And he can't go to his doctor with the story as, owing to his being a minor and how the story would sound, it would likely be reported back to his father and may even lead to a mental health diagnosis. Duncan refuses to go through what his sister did, and his pride will never permit even the *possibility* of his being found mentally ill or deficient.

'It's just some sort of odd drug-induced amnesia,' he tells himself. 'That thing Dad was exposed to, but he gave me the cure before it could do any real damage.'

But by the time he gets to school on Monday, he's so anxious to know what the others experienced that he arrives fifteen minutes early. His anxiety only heightens when he realizes that neither Samantha, nor Michael or Alice, appear to be coming to school today. He almost decides to leave, afraid that he'll be unable to cope with a day of schooling and pretending that everything is okay. And then, right when the bell rings for everyone to report to their first period, he sees Alice and Michael come in from the lot.

There's definitely something wrong. Alice's face is red and she's walking quickly, as if trying to get away from Michael, who's on her heels, speaking with an elevated voice, yet unable to illicit a response from her. Duncan tries to catch up to them as they race to one end of the school, but is unable to close the gap. He shouts their names, but neither seems to notice, and they enter the same classroom. Duncan considers entering the classroom, but decides against it. 'At least they're here. I'll see them at lunch.'

The three periods leading to lunchbreak are agonizing, time slowing to a crawl. Duncan barely gets through the work, delaying as much of it as he can until later. 'I'll catch up when all of this is sorted out,' he tells himself. Lunch break finally at hand, he dashes out to the main courtyard to look for them, ignoring the fact that, due to his being distracted for days, he forgot to grab the lunch that Marie packed for him this morning, and needs to stand in line and buy lunch if he's to eat.

He can't find them, and races around the center and then the periphery of where his classmates congregate in the courtyard. They're not in their typical cool kids spot right in the middle of it all. Panicking, he thinks:

'Maybe they decided to leave.' The thought exacerbates his duress, and he starts to jog through his search, prompting many to gawk at him in wonderment. It's not until he expands his search outside the communal areas that he finally finds them. They're at the very border of the campus, sitting on the curb adjacent to where the buses come to pick up the students without cars.

"Michael! Alice! There you are!," he half-shouts upon approach.

"Go away Duncan!," Michael yells without even looking at him.

"Tell him, he deserves to know," Alice says softly while standing. "We can talk again later, if you insist," she adds before passing Duncan, giving him but the briefest of glances.

"Alice, please!," Michael implores. It's in vain. She's gone. Michael hangs his head as Duncan approaches.

"What's she talking about Michael? What's going on with you two?"

Michael looks up at him with a look of pure enmity, like he's about to spring into an attack. There's such malice in his eyes that Duncan almost backs away, but his determination to shed some light on previous events wins over, and he stays put, asking:

"What? Did I do something wrong?"

"Do you know how many times we've been to that house, Duncan?," Michael asks, now staring into space. His voice is low, but strained, his jaw muscles clenching, as though the only thing containing him is his hold on his own mouth.

"No. Why do you ask? And where's Samantha?"

"We've been there more times than I can count. And yes, Alice smokes and drinks too much, but we've never had any issues until *you* showed up. Then, bam! It's all fucked! I lose my girlfriend! My brother starts acting crazy! Samantha and Caroline are in trouble! All because you have to get your revenge, and show everyone that you're above the football captain and be the man with Sam!"

"Samantha is in trouble? How?"

"Are you listening to me, asshole? Why don't you fuck off and find some other group to make your new friends? Stop plaguing us!"

"I don't know what you're talking about, man. I don't know why you're blaming me for whatever is going on between you two. I can't even remember what happened. That's why I wanted to talk."

"You don't remember, huh? Why is it that I don't believe you? I know what your father does, okay? You can stop playing innocent. And you just happen to show up where me and Alice and Jake hang out on Friday nights the day after Jake insults you in front of the whole school? And now he's scared shitless and doesn't want to talk to me! You made your point, okay! You have all the power! You can destroy people and there's nothing they can do about it, because you don't obey the rules, just like your bad-ass pops! Maybe now you'll have me killed, right? But, honestly, I don't really care right now. This... *pain*..."

Michael hangs his head, then turns his face away. He starts to sob. Duncan is flabbergasted. He doesn't know what to say. He needs to know about Samantha, but this emotional tirade and attached accusations have thrown him for a loop. 'How do I handle this?', he wonders to himself. Attempting to empathize, he thinks of how horrible it would feel to have Samantha and then lose her. He sits down on the curb next to him.

"Michael… listen… you have to believe me man… I don't know what happened, not really. But I swear that I didn't go to that house looking to cause trouble, and that I would never hurt you or anyone else. In fact… I don't know if I should tell you this, but I was at that house because I *don't* know my father… I followed him there."

Michael turns his head and faces Duncan. His eyes are bloodshot and pooling with tears. He says nothing, so Duncan continues.

"It *was* based upon that incident last week at school. But it's not like you say. It's not me… flexing my muscles, or whatever. Actually… what happened with Jake, and then I talked to Alice and she hinted that people are afraid of me because of my father… *I had to know.* So I found out where he was going that day, and I ended up there. I had no idea that you guys are somehow... *connected*. I still don't understand at all. I couldn't find him, and then Samantha spots me, and suddenly I'm partying with the girl of my dreams."

Michael stares at him, searching his eyes. "You swear?," he asks.

"I swear to God, man. Do *you* know what my father does?"

Michael looks away. Seconds pass, as though he's lost in thought. He takes a series of deep breaths, then wipes his eyes with the sleeve of his football team hoodie. The pride usually associated with the garment is gone.

"I know very little," he finally says. "My dad told me to be careful around you, because your father works for... what was the term he used? A *drug kingpin*, I think he said. He wouldn't tell me anything else. But I never suspected your dad was associated with anything that was directly connected to my family... until you just said that. I just thought my dad knew about him because of his own connections. But my brother... he seems to know more. He was ultra-paranoid when I told him you were outside, before you came in. It scared him for some reason. At least that's how I remember it... the little that I *do* remember. But I can't be sure. All of a sudden I don't trust my own memory. Dan, though... I think he's actually working with my father. It has something to do with that place across the street; the place that's connected to my brother's support system and studies at the college. But... again... I don't know what that has to do with your father. But... speaking of my brother... I wasn't going to tell you this because I was pissed at you, but he wants to talk to you, actually. He called me and asked me to tell you to come pay him another visit."

"Okay..." Duncan manages.

"But, I have to warn you... about my brother. Dan isn't... entirely mentally stable, especially when he decides not to take his meds, which he sometimes does. Or if he's been drinking. And sometimes he thinks he's still at war, like he's actively experiencing flashbacks that he can't separate from reality. Whenever he's scared or stressed it gets much worse. Apparently his PTSD can be so bad that it leads to borderline psychosis. So... if you go to see him, keep that in mind. And please don't make it worse. He may ask for your help... so be cautious..."

"Okay... I think I can do that. But you haven't told me about Samantha... she's in trouble? And were we, like, hooking up that night? I have memories of kissing her, but..." he suddenly feels embarrassed, and hesitates before continuing... "but, honestly, I've fantasized about hooking up with her for so long, and my memory of that night is so... hit and miss... that I'm not sure it was real."

"Yea, I think you two were going at it," Michael replies. "But, like you, my memory of

Friday is... *unreliable*. That's part of the problem I'm having with Alice. It's why she decided to break up with me..."

"What do you mean?"

"She thinks I did something to Samantha to get her sick. It's insane! I can't believe her, even when I try to pretend to believe her, and she thinks I'm calling her a liar. But, c'mon! Samantha is sick because she was in contact with her sister. That I *do* remember. Her sister was sick before we even showed up. How am I to blame for that? Plus, I'm pretty sure Alice cheated on me. I keep seeing her kissing someone in my head... some big guy. I think it's someone that lives there. It might even be that guy George. But his girlfriend wouldn't have allowed it, and she must've been there. But I swear it happened!," he screams with frustration. "But Alice, she says that she'd never do that. She thinks I'm calling her a slut and making things up to get out of what she says I did to Sam."

Duncan experiences an odd moment, as though something is trying to bubble up to his consciousness, but is being blocked.

"Do you remember anything like that?," Michael asks, reading Duncan's facial expression.

"Not... *really*."

"What? You're acting like you remember something," Michael presses.

Duncan has a flash of Alice making out with someone. And of Michael being enraged and saying something to Samantha before she goes running upstairs to see her sister Caroline. And of running down the street naked. But the flashes are vague, more like impressions of something real than anything concrete; like he watched them happen on a documentary or something, as a part of someone *else's* life. So, not wanting to make things worse, he refrains from sharing them.

"I don't know… that almost rings a bell," he says, "but the ring is so… *distant*. But, about Samantha, how do you know she's sick?"

"I guess Alice talked to her just before she took her sister Caroline to the hospital on Saturday."

"To the hospital?"

"Yea, apparently she's deathly ill. There hasn't been a hospitalization for COVID in this area for a while now, but that's what it looks like. And somehow she isn't responding to the vaccine that she'd already taken, or to any increased dosage. It looks bad, Alice said."

"Fuck… and Samantha has the same thing?"

"I guess. I mean, I don't know if Alice has talked to her since Saturday, but it makes sense, doesn't it?"

Suddenly it clicks. 'That liquid my dad made me drink!,' Duncan thinks. 'Somehow Samantha's sister was exposed to the same mutated vaccine-resistant form of COVID! But why? How?'

He jumps to his feet. "I have to make a phone call!," he announces. "Hang in there Mike, she'll come around! We'll figure this out!"

Duncan walks quickly away, around the perimeter of the school where he knows he can retain some privacy. He calls his dad's cell phone, but it immediately goes to voicemail. He then places a call to his dad's office, expecting to have to convince the secretary, Grace, to give out more information, but unsure how he'll convince her again.

"Mills and Associates, this is Jeremiah, how may I help you?," comes the voice on the other end of the line.

"Jeremiah..? May I speak with Grace, please?"

"Mrs. Hampton no longer works here, but perhaps I can help you?"

"No longer works there? Why?"

"I'm sorry sir, but I'm not at liberty to divulge personal information without expressed consent."

"Okay... I... I need to speak with my father, Mr. Mills."

"Mr. Mills isn't here at the moment. Shall I take a message for you?"

"No, thank you. This is urgent. Can you tell me where he is, please?"

"I believe he's visiting a client, sir."

"I need to know where!," Duncan demands, feeling his frustration mount.

"Is this an emergency, sir? If so, perhaps I can have one of our lawyers relay a message to him?"

"Yes, please tell him I need to speak with my dad immediately."

"May I know what the nature of the situation is, sir?"

"Just... tell him to tell my dad that I need some more of that stuff that he gave me," Duncan says, immediately regretting saying so, sensing he's done something wrong.

"*Stuff*, sir?" He hears Jeremiah whisper something, as if speaking to someone else, but it's unintelligible. A few seconds later someone else is on the line.

"This is Mr. Donovan, a partner here at the firm. Is this Duncan?"

"Yes…"

"What… *stuff* are you talking about, Duncan?"

Duncan says nothing, unsure how to respond, feeling as though he's somehow said too much already. "Never mind," he finally says. "Just please have my father call me as soon as he can." He hangs up.

"Mother fucker!," he screams aloud to no one. 'This is ridiculous. How can he be unreachable? What is he, like, on a top secret clandestine mission at an undisclosed location or something?'

Duncan unconsciously starts moving towards the parking lot, his mind bouncing between

possible responses to the circumstances.
'Maybe he left that little bottle at the house,'
he thinks, running the short distance to the
parking lot and jumping in his car.

"Hey! Hey, where are you going?," he hears
as he slams the Prius' door shut, barely
having heard the principal, who continues to
yell at him as he backs out of the spot and
screeches out of the lot.

He makes it back home inside eight minutes,
a new record, but he doesn't notice. To his
surprise Marie is there when he bursts
through the front door. She's on her cell
phone in the kitchen, standing over some
papers sprawled across the table.

Duncan freezes. "What are you doing
home?," he asks her. "Aren't you supposed to
be teaching classes?"

She hesitates. Holding eye contact with him, she starts gathering the papers on the kitchen table into one neat stack before replying:

"I'm catching up on some paperwork. I got another instructor to take over for the day. And you? Shouldn't I ask you the same question about your own instruction?"

Duncan shoots forward into the kitchen and begins scanning everything in sight, looking for the little bottle of clear solution.

"What are you looking for, Duncan?"

Hurriedly, he opens all the kitchen drawers and digs through their contents.

"Duncan! I asked you a question!"

"That bottle of COVID treatment stuff Dad gave me… gave *us*. Where is it?"

"What? Why do you need *that*?"

"Just tell me!," he screams. It's the first time he's ever raised his voice to her.

They both stop, staring at one another. Duncan breathes heavily. Marie is calmer, though clearly concerned.

"I... I don't know, Duncan."

He darts over to his father's downstairs study, but the door is locked.

"Please give me the key, Marie."

"I don't have it, Duncan."

He considers trying to break the door open, but decides against it.

"Liar," he says before racing past her and up the stairs, straight into his father's conversion of his brother's bedroom into a second study, Marie close behind.

"Duncan, you're freaking me out, what's going on?"

He scans and starts pushing things around on his father's desk, the one he uses when he works upstairs. He tries to open the desk drawers, but most of them are locked.

"Duncan! Stop it right now! That's your father's private stuff!" She tries to intercede, but he slaps her hand away.

"Duncan!," she screams even louder, her hands going up into what looks like a guard position, her body suddenly wound, as if she's about to defend herself. He's surprised by her athleticism, and the sudden change in her frightens him, like a cougar was just let out of its cage. "I can't believe you just did that!," she shouts.

'What is this?,' Duncan thinks. 'Karate or something?'

He thinks of their bathroom, a reasonable place to put it; maybe in the medicine cabinet. He attempts to pass her, but she steps in front of him. He tries again, more forcefully this tIme, trying to push her aside. In an instant she has him in some sort of hold, one arm around his neck, one of his arms helplessly extended behind him, ready to snap. He feels completely immobilized. 'She's strong as hell,' he thinks.

He stops for a few seconds, but then feels a burst of pride. He tries to wriggle out of her hold, but it only makes things worse, his arm feeling like it may soon snap at the elbow, his neck tightening, throat burning.

"If I let you go, will you relax?," she asks.

"I need it..." he gasps.

She releases him, holding him at arm's length, her palm on his chest. He gasps for air before bending over, trying to fill his lungs.

"It isn't here," she says coolly.

Duncan stands straight up, looking at her in shock and disbelief.

"How do you know that?"

Marie says nothing, only stares at him. She doesn't look angry, but dispassionate, her blue eyes a placid seascape.

"Where is he?," he demands.

"I don't know that either, Duncan," she says flatly.

Infuriated, Duncan darts out of the room, down the stairs and out the front door, Marie yelling behind him: "Duncan, please tell me…"

He sits in his car, chest heaving, trying to process what just happened, and to conceive of the next step. 'Michael said that Dan seems to know about the situation. If Dad's office won't tell me where he is and who this client is, maybe Dan can.'

Duncan takes off in the direction of Apple Blossom Lane. In his rearview Marie stands in the street, imploring him to stop, watching him drive away.

Chapter 6

Nearing 6160 Apple Blossom Lane, the first thing that Duncan notices is the black Lincoln Town Car. It's parked illegally just before the stop sign at the end of the last line of homes bordering the campus, partially hanging into someone's driveway, obstructing the sidewalk. Mr. Romero, the massive man that picked his father up last Friday, is leaning against the trunk, smoking a cigarette.

He sees Duncan drive up. With nowhere to park, Duncan leaves the car on idle on the right side of the street, a few car lengths from TRACE, ten lengths from Romero. Exiting the Prius, he nods at Mr. Romero just before crossing the street. Mr. Romero doesn't nod back or acknowledge him in any way; he doesn't move an inch, in fact, just watches Duncan like a hawk watching a rodent whilst alighted on a branch, his eyes zeroed in.

Duncan knocks on the front door to 6160. No response. He knocks again. Again, no response. He waits a little bit, then decides to try to enter. It's unlocked. He enters the small foyer and closes the door behind him.

There's an odd odor in the air, triggering a memory. 'There's some sort of connection between this place and strange scents,' Duncan thinks. It smells like a mixture of pine trees and gasoline. Coughing, he swings to the right towards the back of the home, stopping when he hears music playing to his left, where the living room is. It sounds like techno music. *Familiar* techno music. Turning left, he circles into the living room, finding all four remaining residents, Dan, Mia, Greta and George, everyone but the recently hospitalized Caroline, sitting on the couch facing the TV. *They're completely still.*

Glancing at the TV, credits are rolling from a recently completed film, a song familiar to

Duncan playing in the background. 'I used to listen to this… is that Moby?,' he wonders. A chill runs up his spine. All four of them are locked in place, just watching the credits.

"Hello?," Duncan half-whispers, afraid to startle them.

No response. 'They're just… *sitting there*,' he thinks, his heartbeat rapidly accelerating.

He steps forward slowly, to the right of the couch, so he can look them in the face. *Horror grips him*. Their eyes are bloodshot, and they're all sitting the same way, staring straight ahead at the TV, their hands clasped in their laps. They seem entirely unaware of him.

'What… the… fuck..?'

"Hello?," he says again, louder this time. They don't even look at him. It's like they're in a trance, completely oblivious of their surroundings. He draws nearer, approaching Dan, who's seated on the right side of the couch closest to him. He waves his hand over his face. No response. He snaps his fingers. Again, no response.

Suddenly, from an unknown source, a loud piercing whistle fills the air. It's so loud and high-pitched that Duncan drops to his knees, covering his ears with his hands in the attempt to shield himself.

The whistle continues for a good ten seconds, Duncan finding his way to his feet, his hands remaining clasped over his ears as he begins to flee the premises. But just as he reaches for the handle of the front door, the auditory bombardment stops. He shakes his head and gets his bearings, then slowly returns to the living room.

All four residents are now on their feet, still staring straight ahead. Then, out of nowhere, Dan shoots to the right, startling Duncan, who falls back against the wall before inching his way back towards the front door, terrified. Dan's half-running with a left-legged limp that looks worse than it was before. The other three residents all put up their right hands, using their pointers and thumbs to form fake guns, like kids at play. Seconds later and they're pursuing Dan towards the back of the house.

Duncan is mesmerized. He considers going after them but, out of fear, finds himself frozen in place. He leans to the right to see what he can see, just as Dan comes bursting around the corner, half-running, pulling the limping left leg, the others close behind him.

Dan is bearing down on him, moving towards the front of the house, and yet doesn't look at him, as if still unaware of his presence. Duncan half-expects to be attacked, and puts up his fists. But Dan moves past him and begins limping up the stairs. A moment later and the other three are climbing the stairs, fake guns still formed in their right hands. Not one of them looks his direction.

"Hello!," Duncan finally finds the courage to shout as they move around the corner and out of eyesight on the second level. 'Is this some sort of performance art or something? What do they call it..? Cosplay, maybe, but without the costumes?' "I'm looking for my dad! I think that his car is parked outside!"

Someone yells something Duncan can't understand, then someone else, then the last one; everyone but Dan, he thinks. But it's in another language. Russian, maybe? 'If they're fucking with me, they're definitely committed.'

Tentatively, Duncan climbs the stairs. He hears some banging, like someone is opening and then slamming drawers closed. Looking around the corner to the left, he sees everyone but Dan gathered outside a doorway. They have their backs to the wall, fake guns still in hand, their attention on the doorway. It looks like they're cops preparing to enter a room, anticipating a firefight.

"What the fuck are you guys doing?," Duncan yells.

Again, no answer. Mia, Greta and George whisper to one another, then all three of them enter the doorway and begin yelling. A moment later and there's a series of loud crashing noises. George comes flying out of the doorway and slams against the opposite wall before collapsing to the ground. He appears unconscious, but whether or not he's faking it, Duncan can't tell. He has no clue of what to make of the exhibition. 'Are they, like, doing some sort of reenactment?'

Duncan runs down the stairs and out the front door. 'Should I, like, get help?,' he wonders. 'What would I say? Hello, 911? Some people that I think I know appear to be play fighting too roughly...'

He looks to his left. Mr. Romero is still leaning against the hood of the black Town Car, smoking a cigarette, staring at Duncan. Looking straight ahead, Duncan zones in on TRACE. 'Maybe they can help,' he thinks, 'with *both* situations.' He starts to sprint across the street, immediately hearing the sound of footsteps converging upon him. Turning back and to his left, he sees Mr. Romero chasing after him, his hand beneath the jacket of his suit, going for the gun hidden on his right hip.

In a panic, Duncan bursts through the front door of TRACE, startling the female secretary seated behind the front desk, who lets out a little shriek, stopping Duncan in his tracks. Mr. Romero is but a moment behind him, coming through the open doorway and putting his hands on Duncan before he can turn around. He just makes out two men behind a glass window in a room behind the shocked secretary, both of whom look familiar. He notices that they're wearing headsets, and seem to be cued in on a computer monitor. *Then the pain.*

Romero's hands feel like vice grips, locking on the trapezius muscles between Duncan's shoulders and his neck with such ferocity that Duncan's knees go weak and the blood to his brain is halted. As darkness descends upon him, he hears a calm, clear command.

"Let him go, Mr. Romero."

The daylight starts to come back, ever so gradually.

"Put him on the couch, please."

He's off his feet in an instant, like a hung shirt being moved to the closet, transported to the couch in the corner of the large room. Coming to, a man is kneeling next to him. He recognizes him immediately. It's Christian Carpenter, the CEO of TRAC whom he'd researched online. Both his demeanor and his attire reminds Duncan of the documentaries that he's seen on the Sicilian Mafia; a fine, navy blue silk suit with a white shirt partway unbuttoned, showing a slight profusion of black chest hair, his face as granite as Romero's whole form, his eyes frigid and all-knowing. Looking around the reception area of TRACE, Duncan realizes that it looks much like 6160, except that it's been retrofitted to serve as an office. The receptionist, seated nearby, seems frightened. Her eyes are closed, and she's forcing herself to take deep breaths. In the large office behind the receptionist one of the two men remains glued to the computer monitor, throwing an occasional glance at Duncan. Again he seems familiar, but Duncan can't quite place him, only associate him with embarrassment.

Mr. Carpenter must've been the other man watching the monitor. Now he's staring at Duncan with an expression of steely inquisitiveness. Duncan goes from imagining an Italian mafia don to a cyborg performing an analysis of a problem to be solved. Mr. Romero is standing directly behind his boss, towering over him, scowling down at Duncan. Full feeling returning, Duncan realizes that Carpenter's fingers are on one side of his neck. He's taking his pulse. Duncan makes eye contact with him. His pulse quickens. Those eyes... so uncaring, yet so discerning. Duncan is suddenly overcome with fright, like he's in danger. Carpenter seems to read this, his eyes reflecting the registration. He smiles ever so slightly.

Duncan tries to sit up, but Carpenter stops him with his other hand, keeping the fingers of his left hand on his carotid artery.

"Now, now, just relax," Carpenter says. "I need to make sure you're okay." It doesn't sound like a request, but an order.

"You're Mr. Mills' son, right? Duncan, is it?"

"Yea… I mean, yes, sir… How did you know?"

Carpenter repeats the sly, subtle smile. "Habit. I worked in intelligence. We make it a point to know everything that we can. You never know when a piece of information may become… *actionable*. I've also been to your home several times, perhaps you remember?"

Duncan tries to remove Carpenter's fingers from his neck. He applies a little force at first, but Carpenter's fingers won't budge. Looking into Carpenter's eyes, he finds that they're searching his own. Duncan suddenly feels naked; vulnerably exposed; seen too clearly. He gets up the courage to apply a little more force. But it's like Carpenter doesn't even notice, or doesn't care. His fingers remain right where they are. Carpenter's eyes move about Duncan's face, as if he's drawing a detailed mental map. Duncan gets a movie flashback in his mind of an artificial lifeform assessing an intruder using facial recognition software. Only when Duncan finally decides to use both hands to push Carpenter's fingers away does Carpenter finally move his hand.

"Now, Duncan. Would you mind telling me why you're here?" Carpenter's eyes remain locked on his. Duncan feels a chill.

"I was looking for my dad," he finally responds, sitting up. "He's not answering his phone, and his office won't tell me where he is."

"Why are you looking for him? Is something wrong?"

"Yes. Please... do you know where he is?"

Carpenter's emotionless eyes move about Duncan's face, then off to one side, then back on Duncan's face. He looks just as he did on the TRAC company website. 'This guy belongs in a sci-fi film,' Duncan thinks. 'A cold,

    The House on Apple Blossom Lane

calculating computer programmed to kill. A real life version of the *Terminator*.'

"Your father is doing some very important work for us at the moment, Duncan," Carpenter says while standing. "I'm afraid he can't be bothered for a while. But perhaps it's something that I can help you with? As your dad's friend, I would be happy to help."

"No, that's okay," Duncan replies. He knows for certain that he can't trust this man. But he doesn't want to *sound* like he knows that.

"Okay. Well, I'm sorry about Mr. Romero here. He's a little protective of me. He didn't hurt you, did he?"

"No, not at all," Duncan lies.

"Perhaps we should drive you home anyway, just to be sure. I would hate to have you get dizzy on your drive back. Your dad would never forgive me if I let you go and you got in a wreck. We'll find somewhere to store your car, and can drop it off at your house tomorrow before school. You *are* supposed to be at school, yes?"

"No thanks... I'll be fine. And yes, I'm normally at school right now. I just... really needed to talk to my dad about something. Something... *personal*."

Duncan stands and starts to walk towards the front door. He only makes it a step before Mr. Romero steps in his way. Carpenter gives Mr. Romero the slightest of head shakes 'no,' barely perceptible, and Mr. Romero gets out of his way. Duncan is terrified, but doesn't want to betray his emotions, worried that they might endanger him somehow. So he manages a "Thank you, sir" while exiting.

He hurries to his vehicle, still idling in the lane, while trying not to *look* like he's hurrying. It takes all the willpower he has not to look back up at TRACE before driving off.

 The House on Apple Blossom Lane

He wants to race away, but doesn't. It's only when he makes it a few blocks that he lets out a massive sigh of relief. 'Have I even been breathing?,' he wonders.

While driving away, back to home or back to school, he's not really sure, and doesn't really care, simply glad to have escaped the lion's den, his mind churns through the events since he parked his car. 'God, I was so scared that I forgot to even mention to them what was happening across the street! But why is it that I feel like that's a good thing? Carpenter definitely doesn't seem like Mr. Compassionate, ready to help. I wouldn't be surprised if he's somehow responsible for it. But how? Why?'

Soon thereafter, Duncan finds himself parked in front of his house, and yet is unable to recall how he got there, as if it wasn't really him that drove home. He sits there, Prius still running, gathering his nerves, thinking of how chilling that series of experiences was.

'I'm not sure which was worse, them sitting there like zombies and running around as if I wasn't there, or being assaulted by that beast of a man and interrogated by his... Beelzebub of a boss. That guy... just his... *presence*. It was like being in the company of the Devil...'

Finally calming, he considers his options. He remembers that, before that last fright, he was determined to find his father. 'Samantha is in trouble!,' he thinks. 'And her sister. I have to be the one to help her. I may be the only one who can.' He imagines getting to the hospital with a cure for Caroline just in time, and Samantha loving him forever for it. 'But how do I find Dad?'

He looks up at the house, wondering if Marie's still home, and could help in some way. 'Something's off with *her* too. She almost tore my arm off! All of sudden it's like there's no one I can trust! No one that's even themselves!' He feels his eyes start to well with tears. He thinks of his mother. He thinks of how things used to be, when the family was together. When his sister was entirely sane. When his dad was stressed, but desperately in love. When his big brother gave him shit constantly, and how it used to piss him off, but now he'd give anything to have him here giving him more shit. The tears start to fall. Then he thinks of Samantha again.

Suddenly a burst of pride, then anger. His mind flies back down Apple Blossom Lane. 'That asshole said Dad's doing something for him. Maybe he's close by. Maybe he's in the TRACE office, or...'

The previous Friday flashes into his mind. He sees Dan eyeing him suspiciously from the back yard, then drifting off to the right... 'The right! That other driveway! That little unit in back! What if... what if that's like TRACE? What if it's another office? That's my best bet, that he's working in there for some reason, or that Dan might know where I can find him, assuming they're over that... *play* of theirs. '

Ten minutes later and he's approaching 6160 again, but much slower than before. He parks his car a block away so that he can approach on foot, surreptitiously. The last thing that he wants is Mr. Romero bearing down on him again. 'He could've crushed me with his bare hands, I know it,' Duncan frets. 'And I may not survive another interrogation by that psycho. So proceed with caution.'

Creeping up to the house, Duncan again sees the black Town Car parked nearby, but this time there's no sign of Mr. Romero, or anyone else. Duncan sneaks around the fence on the left side of the 6160 lot until he's in the backyard. 'I don't think anyone saw me,' he says to himself. Noticing a back window slightly open, he sneaks over to peer inside. "This is a national security emergency," he hears, "we have an imminent threat."

All four residents are gathered around the kitchen table. George is speaking, and it appears as though he's directing everyone else, who pretend to be typing into keyboards while listening to him. Everyone is scraped and bloodied, especially Dan, who has a large gash on the left side of his head, just above his scar. Blood has trickled down the side of his face and begun to crust, but he doesn't seem to mind, or even notice. He looks to be entirely transfixed by George. Duncan watches the reenactment, thinking: 'I know I've seen this before.' That's when he hears an odd whirring sound to his left.

Following the sound along the back wall of the home, Duncan attempts to pinpoint the source. He soon realizes that it isn't coming from the house at all, but from the granny unit in the back right corner of the lot. Suddenly remembering that he's there to find his father and the vaccine, he pulls himself away from the play and approaches the small secondary unit. He looks to his right as he moves towards the unit, peering across the street at TRACE to make sure that no one is watching him. Drawing near to the unit, it's soon clear that it's not another residence. Odd noises are being emitted from behind the door, which looks to be secured not by a typical lock and key configuration, but by something high tech. There's a security card reader, at least that's what Duncan imagines it to be, as well as a camera set above and to the right of the door. To the right of the card reader a small sign reads: "TRACE Storage."

'Shit, now they know I'm here for sure!,' Duncan thinks. He pushes down on the door handle, but it's locked. It doesn't move at all. 'Definitely not a normal lock.' He moves around the left side of the unit. It's about the size of a small one story studio. Yet there are no windows whatsoever and, as he completes one circuit around it, he learns that there's only the one door. He knocks.

"Dad," he half-whispers. "It's me, Duncan, I need to talk to you." Nothing. "Dad!," he says louder, "please, it's really important."

Hearing footsteps behind him, he turns to see Mr. Romero walking quickly in his direction. 'Shit! Not again, please!' Blood pressure spiking, he runs towards the back door of 6160 and, luckily finding it unlocked, bursts through. He slips and almost faceplants on the kitchen floor before finding his footing, turning around and slamming then locking the back door behind him.

"Will you commit to this program?," he hears one of the reenacting residents say. They're no longer in the kitchen, but sound as though they've moved to the living room. Looking out the back window, Duncan sees Romero. He's stopped pursuing him, acting as though he's unable or unwilling to come into the house. No key? 'Like he needs one... dude could probably tear the thing off of its hinges.' Romero mirrors Duncan's movement from outside, eyes locked on Duncan like lasers fixed on a target. Duncan watches him for a moment. They lock eyes. Romero's stare is fierce, like he wants nothing more than to burst into the house and tear Duncan's arms from his sockets, requiring immense self-control not to do so. "Welcome to the program," Duncan hears.

While it takes all his courage and willpower, Duncan turns his back on Mr. Romero and walks into the living room. Dan is standing, pretending to be holding a gun pointed at Greta, who is slumped in one of the living room chairs, appearing to play dead. Mia and George move towards the living room table and start to pound upon it. Dan reacts by spinning around and running up the staircase, the others soon pursuing. As before, they seem not to notice or care that he's there.

Their pounding on the table having drawn his eyes to it, Duncan notices that there's a sheet of paper on it along with four empty, toppled plastic bottles with bright yellow labels.

Picking up the paper, it reads:

"Trauma Research and Counseling Course 107: Reprogramming Traumatic Memories. Professor Gilbert. Extra Credit Assignment: Recall Reborn. Theory: While we have the impulse to bury painful memories in order to protect ourselves from their negative emotional impact, this self-protective tendency can backfire and become detrimental in the long-run, leaving pain unprocessed and able to attack our emotional and psychological wellbeing whenever it's triggered. Exploring traumatic memories in detail allows us the possibility of eventually understanding their impact upon us and processing their meaning in a healthier manner, permitting us to take control of them. One means of accomplishing this feat is through the reenactment."

The paper continues: "Assignment: Gather in your preassigned groups of five. Watch the film *Bourne Ultimatum* from start to end, putting yourself in the position of the characters, especially the main character, Jason Bourne. Attempt to imagine how he feels. When the film is completed, drink your natural memory enhancement shakes, then watch the film again. After completing the film for a second time, reenact the film from start to end to the best of your memory. Reenactment rules: (1) You must stay in your domicile. (2) Skip the reenactment of all car scenes." Where it looks to have said: "(3) No physical violence permitted," the rule is crossed out in black ink, and handwritten next to it, it says: "No physical violence causing severe injury." Also crossed out: "(4) When the reenactment is completed, sit down and share your experience with your peers, comparing how you felt the first time as Jason Bourne, and how you felt after the reenactment." Instead it's written: "When the reenactment is completed, go to your

                    The House on Apple Blossom Lane

room and rest. You'll forget that you've ever seen the film. While you sleep, you'll dream of it, and remember it as a dream."

'Why the alteration?,' he wonders. 'Are they in the advanced course, maybe, and, like, in total focus mode? How could they possibly ignore me *completely*?'

Looking at the back of one of the bottles, Duncan reads the list of ingredients, which include: "Curcumin, Cacao, Resveratrol, Green Tea Extract, Acetyl-L-Carnitine, Ginkgo Biloba and Gotu Kola." Below the bright yellow label is a sticker with handwritten text: "Specially formulated for TRACE Home #37, Seattle WA."

Duncan hears water running loudly upstairs, as if someone has turned on a faucet full-blast, then hears: "Look at us. Look at what they make you give." His fear of them having subsided, especially in comparison to Mr. Romero looming in the backyard, Duncan climbs up the stairs. Near the top he hears a loud splash, and rounds the corner in the direction of the sound. Looking into a bathroom, he sees Dan, fully clothed, splashing around in a full bathtub, water spilling over the sides. George stands in the corner, pretending to hold a gun. Down the hall, he hears two voices, one after another:

"Good morning senators. If I may, I'd like to begin by making a statement for the record…" It's Mia, sitting in a chair in her room, addressing an invisible audience. From the adjacent bedroom he hears:

"After a three day search, Webb's body has yet to be found."

Then, suddenly, silence. All four residents hold their position, looking as they did when Duncan first walked in earlier. Mia and Greta sit at the desks in their room, with George frozen in place pointing his imaginary gun at Dan, who remains submerged underwater in the bathtub. Nearly a minute passes, Duncan feeling as though he might have to try to pull Dan from the tub in order to prevent him from drowning. Finally, they start to move. The ladies, already in their rooms, lay down in their beds, followed by George, leaving the bathroom and walking down the hallway, a dead look on his face, then, soaking wet, Dan drips his way down into his room as well. Again, it's as though Duncan isn't even there.

Uncertain what to do, and remaining seemingly invisible, Duncan eventually decides to follow Dan to his room. He's lying flat on his back on top of his bedspread as it soaks up the moisture from the tub. His eyes are closed. 'God damnit, I need to know where my dad is,' Duncan thinks. Approaching Dan, he gently shakes him, saying:

"Dan, stop pretending. I need to talk to you!"

He doesn't respond. Then a strange smoky smell fills the room, like he's standing in a campfire, but there's no smoke.

Frustrated, Duncan shakes him again, far more vigorously. "God damnit Dan, stop your play for Christ's sake! This is important!"

Dan opens his eyes, staring up at the ceiling, but says nothing. Out of nowhere, Duncan begins to feel sleepy. "D- Dan…"

Kneels buckling, Duncan collapses to the floor and passes out.

Chapter 7

"You? What the hell are you doing here? Why are you... in my room? Hey! Duncan! Wake the hell up!"

Slowly opening his eyes, Duncan turns to see Dan hanging over him. He's lying face down on the carpeted floor of Dan's bedroom.

"I'm... I'm not sure... let me try to remember..." Duncan manages, sitting up and wiping the drool from his face.

"I had some fucked up dreams," Dan says, sitting on his bed and rubbing his temples as Duncan gets his bearings. The recollection of the residents' being in a thriller movie gradually comes back to Dan. What a dream!

"I was… like… an action hero. Chasing people around… trying to solve some sort of mystery… trying to piece together my past… But… it's like it really happened, because I'm sore as hell. Like The Matrix… like my mind made it real or something." He touches the dried blood on the left side of his head, then his swollen lip. His left eye is badly bruised, the flesh a puffy, bluish-purple. "God damn, was I punching myself as I dreamed it?"

"It wasn't a dream," Duncan states. He remembers the reenactment; the sheer terror evoked by their moving past him without even acknowledging his presence, an odd, far off look in their eyes throughout, like they were hypnotized. 'But why was I here?,' he wonders, looking around for a clue to kindle the memory.

"What the hell do you mean?," Dan snorts, incredulous. "Yea, right, I'm like an action hero… Schwarzenegger or Stallone!"

"More like Matt Damon."

"What?"

"Jason Bourne. You and your… fellow residents here were reenacting one of the *Bourne* films yesterday."

"Jason what?"

"The Bourne action films, for Chrissakes! You were acting them out, not dreaming about them. What time is it?"

Duncan glances at the clock on Dan's nightstand. It reads "Tuesday: 6:23 am." Out the window the first rays of the rising sun are just beginning to leap over the horizon.

'God damnit, not again,' Duncan thinks. 'What is it with this place?'

"Wait, *what* were we doing?," Dan demands.

"You and the other people you live here with, you were acting like you were characters in a *Bourne* movie. It's some sort of assignment from… TRAC. Something about trauma and memory."

"Assignment? What assignment? What… series? And why are you in my room, damnit?"

"My God, your memory is even worse than mine. I sincerely don't remember why I came here… something about… *your brother*! He told me that you wanted to see me about something… and something else…"

"You say it was a TRAC assignment? Was anyone from across the street here?"

"No… I don't think so… why?" Duncan suddenly recalls meeting Carpenter, being in TRACE across the street, and that brute, Mr.… Romero… stalking him.

"Wait, yes! Maybe. Do you know Mr. Carpenter and his goon?"

"Mr. Romero," Dan states matter-of-factly. "Yes..." He puts his head between his hands. "I never should've agreed to this... I thought that I could help, and maybe get a little better, but it's only gotten worse. Now I remember why you're here... thanks for coming."

"You're... *welcome*, I think..."

"My memory has been... *defective* since Afghanistan. My counselor across the street, Charlie Kaufman, tells me that it's my mind trying to protect me from the stress of repeatedly reliving the trauma. That my mind has gotten used to burying anything that might harm it, and that I'll invent stories to protect me from the pain rather than face it. I *wanted* to believe that Charlie's trying to help me, but I don't anymore... It's all getting mixed up; violent memories blending with

 The House on Apple Blossom Lane

dreams that feel as real as Afghanistan. I don't know what's true anymore."

"Charlie Kaufman? Sir Charles?"

"Yea, how did you..."

"I've met him, Dan, don't you remember? He's the guy who set up that drinking game last week... It didn't go well, that game. Apparently Alice, your brother's girlfriend, cheated on him during it, and now they're broken up because of it."

Dan stares mournfully at Duncan. His face turns red, and tears well in his eyes. "We don't realize how closely connected are our memories and our... *sanity*... until we start to lose one of them," he says, his voice laden with sorrow. "When our memories are incongruent, so too are our thoughts... our mind. When there are gaps in our memories, they get filled... by us, or *for* us. By what we want or fear to be true, or what we're told is true… Something has to fill the gap in reality to make *our* reality. There's no knowing who or what you are or what you're doing without your memory. And mine has only gotten worse since I agreed to take part in this fucking program, and…" he pauses, staring intensely at Duncan, wondering if he should continue. "And to help my dad."

"Help your dad? With what?"

"That's why I wanted to see you… I don't know how much longer I can take this, and my paranoia is getting worse and, obviously, my memory is failing me… seemingly more and more each day… and I don't know who I can trust. I feel like I can't trust my counselor, if what my dad says is true, but I'm not sure I can trust my dad either, if what Carpenter says is true… And I know your father works for Carpenter, so I probably shouldn't confide in you, but… something about you tells me you may be the *only* person that I can trust.

Like you're the only one around me that's here for the right reasons."

"Trust me with what?"

"My mind is... faltering. I don't want to see Charlie anymore, because I feel like things have only gotten worse since he started counseling and medicating me... And I don't think I can keep up with my assignments... I may be on the verge of losing my mind completely, honestly... So I have to tell someone before..." Dan shakes slightly as he speaks, massaging his temples all the while.

"I have no idea what you're talking about, but you might as well tell me," Duncan offers. "Hopefully I can help. But I'm having trouble myself."

"It's a drug front!," Dan blurts out. Standing, he walks over and closes the door before sitting back on his bed. 'A what?,' Duncan thinks, standing and taking a seat at Dan's desk.

"*That's* what your dad is protecting, okay? They're drug dealers. But on a *major* scale... it's a national... no... *international* operation."

'Shit, maybe he *has* lost his mind.'

"They're running drugs for a Mexican drug cartel, okay!"

That rings a bell in the back of Duncan's mind, which slowly resounds towards the front... 'The people my mom was meeting?'

"My dad found out about it somehow. He told me right after I signed up for the TRAC program and was packing to move here. A program that *he* recommended, by the way, like he was looking out for me; like it was motivated by his love for me. But only after I'd been admitted does the truth come out. He just comes into my room one day and

The House on Apple Blossom Lane

unloads this shit on me. He wants me to look for any signs of it, he says… Can you believe that? It's not enough that I almost had to have my leg amputated after shrapnel from that IED took chunks out of it and that I'm walking around with a limp the rest of my life… And that I have severe PTSD and I'm always paranoid people want to kill me, and… that I sometimes have a hard time separating fact from fiction…. But he wants me to *keep an eye out for anything suspicious*. Suspicious! He has no respect for mental illness! He thinks I'm making all this shit up… all this shit I think and feel and… see. It *all* looks suspicious! *He* looks suspicious! A god damn born two-faced politician… I have no idea which face is facing me from one day to the next! He's just like Carpenter! But I'm no fool, Duncan! I won't let either of them use and discard me! I'll find the best way through this… right through the God damn center!"

He's near to shouting, and speaking rapidly. "Slow down..." Duncan is finally able to interject. "What are you saying, exactly?"

"My dad... Donald McAllister... he's a big wig at the state capitol. He investigates potential fraud and abuse of publicly-funded programs. And *your* dad..."

A knock on the door interrupts him. "Dan, what's going on in there? You're loud as hell."

Dan says nothing. He appears frozen in fear, staring at the door as if a monster is menacing him from the other side.

"It's Greta and George. Can we come in?" It's Greta's voice. She sounds agitated, almost angry.

Dan hesitates, then: "Can you come back in a little bit?"

"Please, may we come in?" It's George this time. "We need to talk to you."

Dan hesitates again, then agrees. "Okay, come in."

They spill into the room, Greta first. "Oh…" she says. "I didn't realize you had company. I thought you were talking to yourself… When did he get here? Did he sleep over?"

"Apparently," Dan says.

"Did you…" George begins, before struggling to continue.

"What? Did I what?," Dan anxiously asks.

"Oh for Chrissakes! Did you attack George again last night?," Greta blurts out.

"What! No! And I told you, I didn't attack him last time either, it was some sort of game we were playing! I'm telling you!"

"A game where you assault my boyfriend in front of me?," Greta fumes. "Look at him! His shirt is torn and he has this huge welt..."

"I told you..." Dan begins, before Duncan interrupts him:

"It *was* a game," he says flatly. "Well, kind of... an *assignment*."

"Assignment? What the hell are you talking about?"

Exasperated by the fact that no one can recall the previous day's events, Duncan shoots downstairs to grab the assignment paper from the coffee table in the living room. But when he gets there, he freezes up. There's no paper. There're no empty 'memory shake' bottles either. The room is tidy, in fact. Holding his head, he remembers how their activities had knocked over chairs and pushed the furniture around. Yet, walking the

     The House on Apple Blossom Lane

premises, there are no such signs. The house is immaculate.

'Could I have imagined all of it?,' he wonders. The others have followed him downstairs. He stares at them in horror. He feels the floor beneath him begin to dematerialize, followed by that sickening sense of gravity sucking him into a free fall. 'Am I losing my grip on reality?' All the other half-baked memories inseparable from fantasy start blending in his brain. Like just happening to hook up with the girl of his dreams. And mystery vaccines, and mafia dons, and his dad's girlfriend suddenly being a martial arts master. Maybe it's all a delusion; *all of it*. He starts hyperventilating. 'Could I be… a *resident* here? What *else* have I imagined? Am I already insane?'

The others sense his angst. They seem to recognize the look on his face. "Sit down…" Dan says. "Relax Duncan, everything's okay." He walks over and puts his hands on Duncan's shoulders, consoling him. "You're in a safe place," he adds, helping him sit on the couch.

"He says we were reenacting an action film when he got here yesterday," Dan says softly to the others, as if worried that speaking in a normal volume will be too much for Duncan, and exacerbate his symptoms. "And *that's* why you look and feel like you were in a fight. I feel the same way," he adds, pointing to the dried blood on the side of his face and gingerly touching his swollen left eye. Dan looks around. "Have you guys seen Mia?"

"I think she went to class," Greta says, eyeing both Dan and Duncan suspiciously, as if not believing a word either has said.

A tense silence hangs in the air for a few moments, interrupted by a phone ringing. Dan recognizes the ring tone and hurries upstairs.

'This is so fucked up,' Duncan thinks, sorting through his memories, categorizing them based upon dependability. Greta and George stand beside him with odd expressions on their face, wondering if he's a friend or foe; trying to determine if he's someone to be fought off, or to empathize with.

"What?," Dan screams upstairs. "They couldn't do anything?"

A moment later, Dan walks slowly downstairs. He takes a seat on the bottom step, a look of shocked disbelief on his face.

"What?," George finally asks. "What is it?"

"Caroline's... *dead*," Dan replies. "And Sam's been hospitalized."

"No... God, please no..." Greta half-whispers.

'Sam..? Wait,' Duncan thinks. 'Caroline and Samantha! So that part of it actually happened, at least.' He finally remembers what had so urgently spurred him to head to the house. He was looking for his father! He needed the liquid vaccine! Snapped back into reality, rediscovering his sanity and momentarily feeling guilty that he's celebrating his sanity in the face of someone's tragic death, he soon shakes it off and jumps to his feet, devising his next move. 'It's still early. Dad's still home.'

"What hospital is she at?," Duncan demands.

"Saint Mary's, why?," Dan responds.

Duncan finalizes his plan, then takes a few deep breaths, summoning the strength he'll need to enact it.

"She should never have started selling drugs here," Dan says softly as Duncan steps towards the front door. "I tried to tell her that it was dangerous... that this is protected turf... that she was drawing the worst type of attention to herself from the worst people... people that simply can't afford to have attention drawn to this place. You can't start selling drugs out of another, *much* bigger dealer's house... Wait, Duncan, where are you going?, I need to talk to you about..."

Closing the door behind him to Dan's shouts of protest, Duncan scans the area, locating and then running to his car. Seconds later and he's pulling away from the curb, unaware that across the street Charlie Kaufman watches him out the window, making a call.

Arriving at home just after 7 am, the first thing Duncan notices is the white Cadillac Escalade with "U.S. GOVERNMENT" plates parked in the driveway. His father's girlfriend, Marie, drives a black Escalade. 'Could there be a connection? And what the fuck is going on now? It doesn't matter... all that matters is the vaccine.'

Bursting through the front door, he finds Marie seated at the kitchen table with two men, one of whom holds a notepad. They're all drinking coffee, and are startled by his sudden presence. One of the men reaches for his holster as Duncan rushes into the room.

"Where's my father?," Duncan demands. "No more bullshit Marie, I need to see him right now, before it's too late!"

"Too late for what, Duncan?"

He says nothing. The men watch him intently.

"Duncan, these men are from the FBI. I called them here because… well, because I think that your father is in serious danger."

"I don't have time for this! Dad!," he screams, running through the downstairs and then up the stairs. "Dad!"

"He isn't here, Duncan. He said he had to go into work early…"

"God fucking damnit!," he yells, heading back out the front door.

"Duncan, please stay! We have to get your father to talk before it's too late…"

Fifteen minutes later and he's standing in the lobby of his father's office in downtown Seattle, having sped through traffic lights and just avoided a couple collisions on the way. He's started yelling. Jeremiah, the receptionist that has taken the place of Grace, stands between him and the hallway leading to his father's office. Another man, one of his father's partners, likely the Mr. Donovan that he spoke with on the phone, is in the hallway taking in the commotion.

Jeremiah attempts to placate Duncan: "He's in a meeting. Just wait a few minutes, I'm sure that…"

"Dad! It's Duncan, I need to talk to you right now! It can't wait!," he screams down the hallway, considering shoving Jeremiah out of the way, who mirrors his lateral movements like a defensive back, resisting putting his hands on him for fear of being called for a penalty.

Moments later a speaker on Jeremiah's desk tones: "It's okay, Jeremiah, just let him pass." It's his father's voice. As Jeremiah steps aside and Duncan darts down the hallway, past Mr. Donovan, towards his father's office at the end of the hall, his father's door opens. Duncan freezes. Out steps Mr. Carpenter and Mr. Romero.

Duncan resumes his movement down the hall, but much slower than before, exchanging periodic glances with Carpenter and Romero. An animalistic instinct informs his progression, telling him to be calm, and not to look either of the men in the eye for too long. Their presence makes the office feel like the jungle; like if he makes the wrong move either one of them may well slice his jugular with their claws, then devour him.

"Hello Duncan," Carpenter says as he passes. "It's good to see you again." His voice is firm and calm, sending a chill up Duncan's spine.

Duncan just manages a "hello" in response, barely emitting the sound. "Sorry, gentleman," his father says. "I'll be with you shortly."

As he enters his father's office, he can feel the fear and tension hanging in the air. It's palpable, as if terror itself has materialized in the room, filling the empty space. His father appears to be in shock. He's never seen him like this before. He has bugeyes, and there are red marks on his throat, as though he's been strangled.

"Dad… Are you okay? Did they… *hurt* you?"

"I'm fine, Duncan. I... got into a disagreement with a man on the street, that's all..." He puts his index finger over his mouth as he speaks, signaling Duncan to be quiet; to not say the wrong thing. Duncan can feel Carpenter and Romero lingering in the hallway, but a few paces away. It's likely that they can hear everything.

"Now, what do you want son? You've interrupted a meeting."

Duncan considers backing down, knowing he's endangering himself and his father just being here, much less by making any demands. Then he thinks of Samantha, and her dead sister, and the pain she must feel, and is overcome with the sense that only he can save her. 'There's no way that you can walk away from this. Man up!'

"I'm sorry Dad," he half-whispers, "but I need that vaccine."

"What vaccine, Duncan?" He tries to sound ignorant. His eyes grow larger and he again motions for Duncan to keep quiet, but more forcefully than before.

"I'm sorry Dad, but I… *need* it. My… girlfriend. She's going to die without it."

"I don't know what you're talking about, Duncan. Can we please talk about this tonight, when I get home?"

"She might not last that long. I can't just let her die."

His father glances to the right side of his desk, very briefly, then looks back at him. 'A tell,' Duncan thinks. 'An involuntary reflex.' Examining that side of his desk with his eyes, Duncan sees a card on the table. "TRAC Security Pass," it says. Reaching over, his dad grabs it and stuffs it into his pocket.

"What is that?," Duncan demands.

"What? It's nothing. It's just something that I need for work. I told you to stop with this, Duncan. You're causing… *problems*, son."

"The vaccine, Dad, where is it?"

Again his father glances down at the same side of his desk. Duncan realizes that he's looking at his desk drawer. In one quick movement Duncan shoots towards it and pulls on the handle of the drawer. His father tries to intervene, but Duncan surprises himself by shoving him away. Jonathan Mills falls backwards, partially dropping into his chair, which slides away, precipitating a slow, awkward descent to the ground as Duncan opens and rifles through the drawer. He recognizes the small vial of clear liquid and seizes it as his father gets to his feet and pounces on him. They struggle for possession.

"You can't have that, Duncan! It can't be taken out of here…"

As Duncan shoves his father back slightly, Mr. Romero bursts through the door, moving towards Duncan.

"Please don't hurt him, Romero!," his father pleads.

On an impulse, Duncan stuffs the vial down the front of his pants as Mr. Romero seizes him, lifting him off his feet and slamming him against the wall. Duncan feels a picture frame crack into his spine halfway up his back, the glass breaking. He grimaces in pain as a couple other pictures fall from the wall, one of them an old family photo including his mother. Jonathan Mills jumps on the brute's back in a desperate attempt to save his son, but with one shift of the beast's shoulder he's ejected, falling to the floor as Romero's hands draw towards Duncan's face. Duncan tries to pull his hands away, but it's useless.

"Stop!," Mr. Carpenter commands. Everyone obediently freezes. "Let him go Mr. Romero."

Duncan is lowered to his feet, gasping for breath. For the briefest of moments he surveys the scene. His father appears more feeble and vulnerable than he ever could've imagined possible. Romero's face is red, but he appears otherwise unaffected. Carpenter just stares at Duncan, cold as ice, the slightest of grins creeping across half of his face. It's as though he always knows something that no one else does; like he's five moves ahead on the chessboard. Duncan inches his way past him, even more slowly than before, this time keeping his eyes locked on the man in control of everyone. Carpenter's eyes never leave him. Like staring into the fixed, unyielding gaze of a statue of Satan.

Duncan takes one more look over his shoulder at his father, then strides away down the hall. As his father gets to his feet, pushing his chair back into position before sitting behind his desk, Carpenter closes the door to the office. No one else in the office has taken any action, pretending as though nothing's happened.

It takes him less than ten minutes to get to St. Mary's Hospital, and almost another ten before the receptionist, in league with the head doctor on duty, can be convinced that his assurances of being Samantha's boyfriend are sufficient to grant him entry into the emergency wing in which she's being held under quarantine. Once there he's held at bay by a bevy of orderlies. Behind makeshift plastic sheeting isolating a part of the emergency ward Duncan sees doctors and nurses running in and out of a room, all wearing hazard suits. A man and woman sit holding one another, rocking back and forth just outside the hung sheeting, the woman sobbing. Pulling the vial from his pocket, Duncan demands to see the physician.

"He's trying to save her," a nervous young nurse assures him, her face beet red.

"But he won't be able to without this!," Duncan cries, holding the vial in his hand. This gets the attention of Samantha's parents. The father stands and approaches.

"What is it?"

"It's a vaccine! I know what she has! This is the only thing that can save her life!"

The nurse assures them that they're using all of the means at their disposal. She says that there's nothing *he*, Duncan, has, that they don't have, and that, even if it's true that it's some specialty antidote, the law won't allow them to use it. An argument ensues. The father grabs the vial from Duncan before rushing forward with the mother as one determined team. They push through the plastic, demanding that the vaccine be used, law and protocol and liability be damned.

"It's our daughter!," the mother pleads. "Obviously you don't have anything that she needs! She's only gotten worse since she's arrived, just like her sister! Please, she's all that we have left!"

Two security guards intercede just before they're able to breach their daughter's plastic-tented confines, holding the couple back, Duncan watching from twenty yards away. Then the flap of the inner tent opens. A doctor exits, his head hung. Duncan can't hear what he softly says, but it's obvious. It's over. *Samantha is dead.*

As her mother collapses to the floor at the doctor's feet the father pushes past the doctor, into the room, screaming a moment later. Dizzy, absorbing the pain of Samantha's parents as it collides with his own whirlwind of emotions, he leans against the wall.

'Mother fuckers! Mother fuckers!!!'

Walking briskly back down the hall towards the exit, he calls his father's office. "He's gone home early," Jeremiah informs him.

Tears streaming down his cheeks, Duncan flees the hospital in a rage, feeling more murderous than he ever has in his life. 'Someone will pay for this!,' he thinks over and over. Flying home, he pushes his little Prius to the limit, completely neglecting all traffic laws. Eyes so welled with tears he can scarcely see, he sideswipes a Mercedes driving through one intersection. It's a miracle that he isn't stopped by police.

Nearing his house, he notices the black Lincoln Town Car behind him. 'Those fuckers are following me!' Slamming on the breaks, he exits the car, leaving it idling in the street. Sprinting at the Town Car, it stops. He circles the car, looking through the tinted windows.

He can just make out Mr. Romero in the driver's seat, but can't see through the rear windows at the object of his rage. 'Carpenter and my father's cowardice killed her,' he thinks. 'They won't get away with this shit!'

"Come out!," he yells at the top of his lungs. "Stop hiding behind your thug and come out and face me like a man." No response. Circling the vehicle twice more, he's forced to take out his rage on the hood of the car, slamming both fists into it numerous times, so hard that he thinks he may've broken his hands. He considers doing more, like grabbing a stone and launching it at Romero through the windshield, but finally decides its futile. Sprinting back to his car, he floors it for the final half mile to his house, breaking and screeching to a halt less than a foot from slamming into the garage door.

"Dad! Dad, where the fuck are you?," he shouts as he bursts through the unlocked front door. No response. He sprints into the kitchen. No one. Up the stairs. Also empty. Back down the stairs and into the foyer, fuming. That's when he hears the sobbing.

Walking into the living room, he finds his father on the couch, his face buried in his hands, one of which clenches a sheet of paper. Duncan approaches him, his anger only slightly tempered by his father's emotional state.

"You let her die," Duncan says, his voice wavering. His father says nothing. Barely able to contain his rage, Duncan snatches the paper out of his father's hand.

On the lined yellow sheet a message reads:

"I love you, but I can't stay here and watch you kill yourself for these lowlifes any longer. Call the number on the card I left for you on your desk and save your life, and the life of your son. He's involved now. The FBI has seen him at that house, and they were here today.

As soon as you agree to testify, I'll come back to you. I love you always: Marie."

It's mostly silent for a few seconds, the only sounds the soft sobbing of his father and his own heart beating in his eardrums.

"You don't know these people, Duncan," his father finally manages, his voice low and defeated, as though uttered by the shell of a human being locked in a deep dark dungeon. "They're connected… at the *highest* levels. There's no hiding from them. There's no getting out. If I testify, I'm dead; you're dead; your brother and sister are dead. And even if I *did* testify, it would never be admitted in court. They'd quash it, like they did before. There're simply too many people in too high of places with their hands on the levers of power to permit anything to come of it. Too many big money interests at stake, don't you see? Profit can't afford the proliferation of the truth, son. We'd all die, and all of it would be buried. You're probably dead already. We all are. One wrong move a decade ago doomed us all... Your mother thought we could get out too... she was wrong. She tried, and it killed her. There's no *getting out*, no running from these... *people*, son, only sticking with it, moving through the dark tunnel, hoping beyond all rational hope that somewhere, at the end of it, there's a light..."

"So what are you saying exactly, Dad? That this is the reason that Mom is dead, and why my girlfriend and her sister are dead, and why Marie's decided to leave you, and, what..? You're not going to do anything about it? You're just going to keep on helping them?"

Jonathan Mills looks up at his son. He feels the full weight of the world leaning on him. He's trapped. A shock-treated animal caught in a cage. And now his youngest child is in the trap with him, and if he can't get him out, it may spell the end for them all. He thinks of that horrible online video he saw once, with that family of raccoons on the highway, the traffic continuing to come even as the surviving members of the clan scream at the terror of their loved ones bleeding their last onto the unfeeling asphalt. And he's lost his love, the one person who made it seem like he could find his way through it. His guide. The one person that gave him the strength to keep fighting. But what can he do? Saving his kids is all that matters now.

"Duncan, none of that is true." His voice has changed; gone dead; emotionless. "The vaccine that I gave you had nothing to do with TRACE or Mr. Carpenter. It's an entirely separate matter; a different client. I didn't even know that you had a girlfriend. But there's no way that she or her sister could have been connected. And I... think you may have misunderstood what I just said about your mother... Mr. Carpenter didn't kill her, she got herself killed. She tried to make a deal with the wrong people in exchange for the right to start a new job... to make a new start in a very dangerous part of the world that she felt the need to help, and it backfired."

Duncan stares into the inconsolable eyes of his broken-down father, a man he never thought he could see so dejected; so small. The pain of seeing his father in this state and the rage of feeling like that same father is lying to him battle in his heart and mind, his heart breaking as his blood boils. He's so overwhelmed by it all that he can't find the words. 'This is bullshit,' he finally decides. 'I'm not going along with this.'

"I don't believe you, Dad," he finally manages. "I've spoken with Mr. Carpenter. I've been attacked by Romero. I know that they're responsible for all of this. I can see it in their eyes, Dad, just like I see it in yours, regardless of what you say. And I know that you know it too. I know that you're just trying to protect me, but it's gone too far. It's too late. You have to do something about this, or I will. I won't just sit by and watch them

     The House on Apple Blossom Lane

continue to use you. I won't just let them get away with killing people."

His father just shakes his head, repeating "You can't; you can't."

"I have a friend at school, and his dad told him that you basically work for drug dealers."

Jonathan Mills is instantly wide-eyed upon hearing this. He goes from utterly dejected to fiercely determined in an instant.

"What? Which friend? What's his name…?"

"Is it true, Dad?"

In a split second Jonathan Mills is off his feet and has his hands on his son's shoulders, pinning him to the sofa, his sorrow and defeat reversed into a furious force.

"Who told you that, Duncan? Tell me right now!"

"Get your fucking hands off of me!" He tries to fight him off, but finds that he can't. 'I thought I was the angry one,' he thinks.

"Who, Duncan? Who..."

"Michael and his brother Dan..."

"Michael and Dan *what*, Duncan? What's their last name?"

"Mc-something... Mc... *Allister*, I think he said."

"Damnit, I knew it!," Jonathan Mills puffs. He lets go of his son and picks up his cell phone off the side table before pacing back and forth with it in his hand, looking like he's about to explode.

"Is it true, Dad? Do you work for..."

"Listen to me right now, Duncan. I know that you think you understand this situation. And it's clear by now that you refuse to listen to me, no matter what the consequences. But that... *fucking asshole*, Donald McAllister, is going to get you killed. And his own sons killed. And let me tell you something else. *He* is the real bad guy in this situation. He and those he works for. How he could involve his sons in this is beyond deplorable!"

"What do you mean?"

"Listen... Duncan... I know you think the world is simple. Like it's divided between good guys and bad guys. But that's some *Disney* bullshit, son. We *all* have the capacity for good and evil in us at every moment of every day. Good and evil are *choices*, not innate qualities. And when there are fortunes to be made, the bad simply comes out of the people best positioned to make them. The fortunes attract those willing to do whatever is necessary to claim them, understand? They demonstrate that everyone has Satan within them, and everyone has their price and what they're willing to do to grab the wealth and the power. And no matter what McAllister says to his sons, he's no better than the people that I work for. He's just a representative of those competing for the same fortunes, hiding behind different masks. Who better positioned to abuse authority than someone constitutionally-tasked to counteract such abuse?"

"I don't understand what you mean…"

"He's been investigating many of the people and companies that I work for for years, Duncan. We've sued him for slander twice, and one of his investigators for harassment. He's as despicable as they come. He's the type of person that gives politicians the reputation that they have. He pretends to be fighting against evil when all the while he's using his position and his power to take down the competitors of those that finance his campaigns, and whose stock he owns. He's supposed to be an unbiased prosecutor of the corrupt, when he's as corrupt as any of them, and uses his authority to investigate those standing in the way of his financial interests, and the financial interests of his partners. You see? It's like... having your hand plunged into the bottom of the cookie jar whilst pretending to fight diabetes!"

"But..."

"That's enough!," he screams. "I won't say anything else. I've already told you far more than I should've. I'm just... not thinking clearly right now. All this stress..."

They stare at one another for a few seconds, then Jonathan Mills speaks back up:

"I'm getting you out of this right now, Duncan. Your schoolwork is just going to have to suffer. I'm sending you east to stay with your brother and sister, and I don't want to hear another word about it."

"No," Duncan half-whispers a moment later. "No, I won't…"

"Shut up, Duncan! That's enough. I've made up my mind. You're still a minor, and you're going to do what I say."

Jonathan Mills turns from his son and makes a call on his cell phone. A second later: "Donovan, it's Mills. Listen, McAllister is stirring up trouble again, but this time he's trying to hide it behind his kids. We have to take action now, before…"

"Fuck this!," Duncan shouts before sprinting towards the front door, his father close behind him. Swinging the door open, it rams into his father's outreached hand. He yelps in pain and drops his phone, cursing violently as Duncan slips through the opening of the partially ajar door. There's no sign of

The House on Apple Blossom Lane

Carpenter's Town Car. Seconds later he's backing out of the driveway. Jonathan Mills ambles out the door, slamming his son's car with his hands, throwing himself against it while it backs up, trying desperately to stop it with his body. Putting the Prius in drive, Duncan accelerates around his father, missing him by inches, his cries trailing behind him.

Chapter 8

'There's no way that I'm just running away,' Duncan thinks while speeding away from home, on the way to nowhere in particular. 'Not with everything that's happened. There've been too many casualties already, what with Samantha and her sister, and I suspect Mom as well, and now Marie leaving. And Dan is in way over his head... Whatever's going on, it's like a deadly virus. There's no telling how many it'll take. And Dad is too scared to do anything about it. Which means that without... *intervention*, without a push, without some sort of action from me, he's likely to stay on their leash forever. Carpenter will never let him off. I can see it in his eyes. He's all control, all domination, concealed by websites and nonprofit trickery. Should I go to the FBI? No... if what I've heard is right, it won't go anywhere. It'll just be covered up. So who can take them down?'

Head spinning, going through the options, he eventually determines that the best course of action might be consorting with the enemy. Dan's father... this Donald McAllister. 'I have no idea how accurate Dan's take is... how much I can trust that he knows what he thinks he knows, what with his own brother warning me about his instability, and his own admissions of feeling like his sanity is slipping, and all that odd behavior at that house. Shit, man, that house will *make* you go insane, not remedy insanity. I almost lost it there myself. Something very strange is going on there. Maybe Dan's dad can help. Maybe I can read him in some way... find out more about Dan and TRACE. At least he's likely to be motivated to take some action against them.'

Resolving to pay a visit to Donald McAllister, Duncan pulls over and looks him up on his phone. It only takes him a few minutes to find him online. He's Director of Washington State's Office of Financial Fraud and

Corruption, described on their website as "a division of Washing State's Financial Management Department responsible for vetting public partners and investigating white collar crimes connected to public financing." He works out of a complex across the street from the State Capitol Building in Olympia. He feels guilty making the decision, like he's betraying his father, but doesn't see any way around it. 'He'll know something I can use. He'll betray some fact... I just have to be on my guard. Proceed with caution. Play a little poker with him. I may be out of my league, but it's a chance I have to take.'

Soon he's on the I5 headed south towards the capitol. In those moments passing over bridges crossing the manifold inlets into the southern section of the Puget Sound, the drive is gorgeous, almost making him forget his miserable situation. It reminds Duncan of the few family trips around the Olympic Peninsula to the west as a kid; the majestic mountainous bulwark between the coast and urban Washington. Forests so green, so thick with life, you feel like you have to brush it away with your hand to pass through it. Carpets of fern and moss as luxuriously verdant as anywhere on Earth. A true rainforest west of Mount Olympus, with the steadily rising elevation catching hundreds of inches of rain a year and dumping it down its cascading chutes, pouring into its lakes, rivers and forests, supporting more plant life per acre than anywhere else in the ultra-green Pacific Northwest. The Hall of Mosses... an ancient forest of layered life, the plants so well fed and watered they grow in stacks.

Approaching Olympia, a nervous anxiety sets in. 'What if McAllister laughs me out of his office? Or, worse, what if he refuses to see me entirely?' Glancing in the rearview, he swears he sees Marie driving behind him, but she disappears as quickly as she appears. It comforts him somehow, regardless of their recent altercation. 'I'm so desperate for help

that I'm seeing what I want to see… I want
helpers, but there are none. It's all on me.'

Once in the parking lot of the capitol
complex, it takes Duncan a few minutes to
locate the Office of Financial Management,
and, within it, the Office of Financial Fraud
and Corruption, using an onsite map.
Circuitously, he navigates his way through the
assorted edifices through which the state is
managed, or *mismanaged*, if what his father
says is anywhere near the truth. A few people
give him concerned looks owing to his clearly
exhibited distress. At one point he almost
crashes into a *Federal Express* delivery
woman. Finally, his head pounding, he's
looking at McAllister's receptionist.

She's arguing with the same *Federal Express*
delivery woman that he almost toppled on
the way in. 'Obviously she's more efficient
than me. I should've asked *her* for directions.'
Oddly, she looks much like Marie, except that
she has dark, longer hair and brown eyes. It's

            The House on Apple Blossom Lane

like he's seeing her everywhere. 'Maybe I'm comforting myself by pretending like I have allies around me...'

"Fine, if he has to be the one to sign for it, go ahead..." says McAllister's receptionist to the delivery woman.

In the time it takes for the *Fed Ex* woman to drop off her letter, get her signature and leave, Duncan makes his case to the perturbed receptionist that he deserves some of Mr. McAllister's precious time. At first he's assured that Mr. McAllister is unavailable without an appointment. He's very busy, after all. But Duncan is ready for that, and refuses to just walk away.

"Please tell Mr. McAllister that I know his sons, and I think that one of them may be in serious trouble. I think he may be about to suffer some sort of breakdown, or, worse, provoke someone dangerous."

This message gets the earnest attention of the receptionist and, relayed to Donald McAllister, has him coming out to greet him. Mr. McAllister is short and bulky, with silver hair combed back, a well-kept silver beard with the last shreds of black fast losing ground, and blue eyes like his sons', but colder. Even through his slacks and long-sleeved shirt Duncan can tell that his arms and legs, especially his legs, are thick and muscular, like those of a soccer player or bicyclist. Duncan sees the prototypical male power player that carries the muscularity and testosterone built-up on the weights and stationary bike into his personal and professional life, lending him a commanding presence. He's holding a large black coffee mug with the state seal of Washington stamped in silver onto it, as if he chose the mug to match his own look.

"Please hold my calls Lisa. Oh, and Lisa, are you trying a new type of coffee or something?" He stares into his mug, smacking his mouth in a display of disagreeability.

"No, Mr. McAllister, it's the same Costco-brand coffee that we've always used, why?"

"Maybe I just let it get cold. It tastes funny to me. Duncan, is it?," he asks, motioning for him to enter and promptly closing the door behind him.

Duncan enters what he envisages to be a replica of the Oval Office. The place where deals get done. A large square room lorded over by a stately desk, surrounded by all the accoutrement of a person in a position of power.

"Yes, sir. I'll be honest with you, I'm not sure if I should be here."

"That's okay, son. If you're a friend of my sons, and have the right intentions, I'll do everything in my power to help you. Now, what brought you in to see me today? You think my son is in trouble?"

"Yes... I think Dan's in trouble."

"Oh yea, and why do you say that?" He doesn't sound the least bit surprised, as if Duncan is telling him something obvious; something he's long been well aware of. "And how do you know him, exactly?" McAllister's demeanor is one of great composure. It's clear he's spent a lot of time putting out fires, and doesn't flee from the heat.

"Well... I don't know if I should tell you this, but I'm at my wits end. I need help with him, and the whole situation, honestly."

"What situation, Duncan?"

"Some things happened at my high school, where I go to school with your youngest son, Michael. I assume he's your youngest..."

For some reason, this admission provokes a slight alteration in McAllister's affect. It's barely perceptible, but his eyes flash a bit at the mention of Michael's name. Duncan likely wouldn't have perceived it at all had he not prepared himself to read McAllister's reactions. All those hours of watching the poker tournaments and the whole 'read the player, not the cards' thing.

"Yes, he's my youngest son. So you go to San Gabriel?"

"Yes, sir. Anyway, I found out that Mike had a certain... impression of me, because of my father."

Another slight alteration of affect; a narrowing of the eyes and a slight stiffening of the body. But subtle.

"Oh yea, and who is your father, Duncan?"

"Jonathan Mills."

McAllister's composed countenance gives way to the slightest of grins.

"And you're here on your father's behalf?"

"No… not at all. He doesn't even know that I'm here. In fact, he'd scold me severely if he knew I'd driven down here, I'm sure of it."

Duncan gets the sense that the table has been set, and his opponent is now invested in the game, reading him as well. A power has been provoked in that opponent, stirring the energy in the room. Duncan fears that he's outmatched. His pulse quickens. 'What was I thinking? He plays this game for a living…'

"What does this have to do with my son, Duncan?"

"Well, both Mike and Dan seem to think that my father's, like, *evil* or something. That he works for some sort of crime lord, and helps

The House on Apple Blossom Lane

him get away with evil deeds as his lawyer. So, of course this concerns me, but… I don't know how much of it is in Dan's head, because, well… excuse me for saying so, sir, but he *is* being treated for trauma and mental illness."

The young and older man stare at each other for a moment, each searching for a sign in the other on which card to play next.

"Yes, Duncan, I'm afraid that he is. War takes the most horrible of tolls. Even if it doesn't take your body, there's no way for a mind to be exposed to the state of fending off its own violent death without it costing a great deal. Spend enough time feeling like death is imminent, it sticks, and becomes a part of the self-defending psyche. I'm not sure you can ever fully be at peace after that."

As he says this his affect seems to crack a little, with the first sign of emotion surfacing.

But what emotions, Duncan isn't sure. Sorrow? Guilt? Anger? All of these?

"Right… well, again, I'm sorry, sir, but Dan seems to think he's on some sort of mission, and makes it sound like you're the commander. He thinks he's at that house to search for some sort of criminal mastermind, or some conspiracy ring or something, and that you sent him there. And he's targeting those that have power over him, which I assume is natural. He thinks they killed his friend, Caroline, and my friend, Samantha, her sister, and that the people that operate the program that he's in are, like, part of a front for some sort of international narcotics trafficking operation."

As Duncan says this, Donald McAllister opens a notepad on his desk and makes some notations, scarcely taking his eyes off of Duncan. Then comes a long period of silence, to the point of becoming awkward. Duncan feels like Donald is testing him somehow. His nerves give way.

"So, is it true, sir?," he blurts out louder than necessary.

"Is what true, Duncan?" McAllister is calm; steady. There's no chance of him losing his composure. Duncan has lost the hand. The only remaining question is how *big* of a hand he's lost.

"All of it? Any of it? I need to know what to do…"

McAllister stares at him for a few seconds, scratching his chin, attempting to determine his play.

"Let me tell you a story, Duncan. A sad, sobering story sitting atop an incalculably tall mountain of human and financial loss. A tragedy unknown to most."

"Okay…"

"But first, do me a favor. Lift up your shirt."

"Uh…"

"Just do it, son."

Begrudgingly obliging, Duncan lifts his shirt.

"Now turn around for me."

'This is getting creepy. Oh my God, he thinks I'm wired!'

"I'm not wearing a listening device, for Chrissakes!"

But he knows that won't suffice. So he does his spin and, seconds later, lets McAllister examine his phone, which he's forced to leave on the big wig's desk. Satisfied, McAllister sits on the edge of that oversized desk, a piece of furniture that might as well be a trophy, and, leaning forward, with a smug smile on his face, says:

"You're coming of age, and on some level you're a part of a hidden world that's been circulating around you your entire life, even as you've been oblivious to it. And I know that your dad thinks that he's protecting you by keeping information from you, but I tend to think that kids your age are becoming adults, and we need to share certain… *facts* with you in order to keep you safe… So that you, and Michael and Dan, and your friends, have some understanding of how dangerous the world is, so they can think about it for themselves, and steer clear."

'Fuck, he sounds like Dad.'

"The truth is, Duncan, that the War on Drugs isn't what it appears to be. It was never meant to *end* the drug supply. That's just one of the *many* lies sold to the public so that crookery can continue, legal or not. None of

the powers that be that were most
responsible for generating the public support
for that war have ever seriously entertained
the delusion that the supply of narcotics into
the United States can actually be *stopped*.”

Duncan thinks he sees beads of sweat
forming on McAllister’s forehead.

“Like the so-called War on Terror, it’s a war
that was *made* to be endless, fought against
an unknown, unseen, unceasing succession of
enemies. Because when there’s a war against
an invisible enemy, and you can get the
public to agree that it exists and that it’s of
vital importance, it doesn’t end. And so
neither does the public support for and
financing of that war, or the profits that the
war generates; that *all* war generates.”

“Okay…”

“The War on Drugs, like every war waged by
the United States since the end of World War

Two, is a war that was created to *hide* the criminals, and to convince the gullible public that the enemy is *overseas*, embodied by whomever stands against the interests of the domestic kingpins selling that war. It wasn't meant to identify, prosecute or kill those actually *responsible* for the war. Most of those responsible for how that war is waged never really *wanted* the supply of drugs to be stopped in the first place. All that they want is to be the ones controlling it. Why would profiteers want to burn their merchandise, Duncan? Only fools fall for that bullshit. The supply of narcotics represents a *big* part of the seedy underbelly of capitalism. And as long as there's demand, which there always will be, *someone* is going to make a fortune off of its supply, especially if it can be kept illegal, and therefore more profitable. Just look at what's happened to the price of marijuana... Get it?"

"I think so..."

"Do you think the kings and queens of industry, those that make billions a year on the supply of everything else, are just going to sit back and let the gangs and cartels make all those fortunes and buy all the political influence with that money when they have the U.S. Army and CIA at their disposal, and can so successfully sell such profitable intercession as... well, as whatever type of war is easiest to sell to the public at any given time? Do you think a pharmaceutical executive is going to stand up and say: you know what, Mother Nature supplies everything you need, and without dependency or side effects, and at the tiniest fraction of the price we charge, so I've hereby found my conscience and must resign my post paying me ten million dollars a year? It's hush money, son. Billions are spent bribing people to stay quiet across all these shady industries. People in any type of power position are paid for their quiet passivity; for their moral ambivalence. More money is

     The House on Apple Blossom Lane

spent on sealing lips than on skills, actually... See what I mean?"

"Well, I..."

"Just like, do you think any American politician will ever stand up and say: The U.S. Army is actually responsible for more terrorism than those we condemn as terrorists, because terrorism is essentially armed resistance to our imperial penetration of foreign lands, resources and underdeveloped consumer markets? Most will dismiss this as mere cynicism, but, fundamentally, most terrorism is really just resistance to what we call globalization, Duncan. Shit, Al Qaeda was created by the U.S. Government to resist the Soviet encroachment of the Middle East and its oil and poppy fields. Now they resist *our* encroachment, so Americans call them terrorists. We fed and raised the dog and trained him to fight the Soviets in the global dogfight, then the dog slips off his leash and decides that his red, white and blue master is no better than the red dog that he's been fighting, so now we need to put him down."

"I've never heard that one…"

"Because the U.S. Government won't allow it to be taught. It's just one of countless examples of invasion and the countering of invasion with one thing in mind: *money*. There's just too much money to be made by American corporations *not* to act. Everything is a cost-benefit analysis of profit and power, son. *Everything*. It's the same reason that no U.S. politician will ever publicly say: Religion is the history of empires artificially constraining spirituality for the corrupt purpose of controlling the minds of the masses, pretending to stuff spirituality into a pre-packaged, ready-to-sell box in which it'll never fit. When eighty percent of the voting public votes for reflexive flag-waving and cross-wearing, saying any such thing is the same as committing political suicide."

"I never thought of it that way."

"And call me a quack, but I'm with the conspiracy theorists on the 9/11 thing. Motive, means and opportunity just align far too perfectly, especially considering the power players in the upper echelons of government back then, and how they stood to gain; how they *did* gain. It's just way too convenient that 9/11 created the perfect means to push the Patriot Act through Congress, so that those connected to the massive intelligence apparatus operating within the United States Federal Government could gain unrestricted access to every bit of electronic data available. It's just way too convenient that it also supplied the perfect justification for invading the Middle East to finish the job and assuage the ego of the father through his then presidential son, all to the immense profiteering benefit of connected international business interests."

McAllister abruptly coughs three times, loudly. They come unexpectedly, producing spews. Embarrassed, he wipes spittle from his perfectly manicured goatee, the image of perfection having been shattered. But he's on a role and loving the release, so he continues.

"And it's just way too convenient that so-called 'weapons of mass destruction' being 'discovered' in the hands of those old enemies finalized the successful push of that agenda, even as all the evidence has since been found to have been fabricated by those in the Executive Branch, all with impunity. We're supposed to believe that the government being led by former defense contractor corporation big-wigs was a coincidence in all of that? I mean, how much more obvious could it be that 9/11 was a *chosen* date, for Chrissakes? C'mon... 9-1-1. *Obviously* that's a propagandist date selection made to manipulate the fear of the gullible American public, conditioning them to associate the date with emergency so that

   The House on Apple Blossom Lane

the true perpetrators would have the public support to do anything that they wanted, like spy on everyone and everything and send the military in to clear a path for the corporations that came in after them. What's a few thousand American civilians compared to countless billions of future profits and control of the Middle East?"

"Isn't that a bit far-fetched, sir?"

"Not at all, actually. I *fetched it* straight from the investigator's handbook. The rational conspiracy theories are based upon connecting the dots between motive, means and opportunity. Speaking of which, the Patriot Act gave the NSA the perfect excuse to tap into all of the private tech databases, starting with Google and Facebook. Sorry, with *Meta*. That rebranding betrays their intention: meta-tech supplanting metaphysics; the Meta Monster consuming God. The Patriot Act was just the first step in Meta becoming the center of the spying, monitoring and censoring apparatus, as an indistinct extension of the intelligence community. When is the public going to realize that Meta is the real life version of Big Brother? You've read *1984* by now, right?"

"Yea, last year..."

"I think that Orwell was presaging Meta. It's the inextricably deep seated blurring of the public-private line; the inseparable Church and State of our time. A monster feeding off of the people, defending the passageways of moral propriety, dictating what's allowed to be said, pulling the megaphone away from anything and anyone that's at odds with political correctness and the conservative agenda. Is Meta the monster, or is it the NSA? And at what point do people start to realize that the answer is obviously *both*; that, like the politicians, the online police are only *pretending* to serve the people. What they're really doing is collecting and selling their data and helping the government spy and censor and accumulate information that they can use against anything and anyone deemed unpatriotic. And with recent tech toys, it's just a matter of time before the line between Meta and mankind *itself* is blurred, as sci-fi has long predicted. Soon the so-called advancement of humanity will be based upon cyborgs existing as semi-autonomous extensions of Big Brother, having sacrificed their humanity and self-thought. Technology *used* to be an extension of us, but it won't be long before we're more an extension of *it*."

"That sounds a little nuts, sir, I'm sorry to say…"

"That's exactly what they *want* you to think, my dear boy. From my experience, it's all about the opportunity to profit. It makes monsters, I say, even of good people!"

"What are you saying, exactly?"

"I'm saying it's all an inside job by those with the motive, means and opportunity to profit on a global scale; in the *big* game. Everything that I've been talking about makes *billions* for those pulling the highest political strings. Especially considering that the American People are the ones paying most of the bills! We cover most of the expenses! Just like we financed the 2008 bailouts after their sheer insider greed capsized the economy."

"But what does this have to do with TRAC, sir?"

"Everything, Duncan. This is why they exist: *profit over people*. You think that the most effective drug policy, what's in the best interests of the most people, legalizing, taxing and providing safe havens for the use of narcotics, and plowing all the proceeds into cultivating public benefits, like empowering bigger insurers to force those pharmaceutical companies to charge the public less, will actually happen? You think that those making unfathomable fortunes do anything other than conceal such things? You think the profiteers actually *care* about the people? Politics, Duncan, is about saying what the public wants to hear while on the podium whilst finding ways to steal and profit off of them behind closed doors like mine. It's about putting on a patriotic puppet show with your left hand whilst plunging your right hand into public coffers."

This admission that he's part of the problem seems to be a relief to Donald McAllister, who smiles as he says it. It's as though he's always wanted to say it out loud. Like he *needed* to say it. Meanwhile, Duncan's head spins. He just wants out of his own situation. Saving the people was never on his mind. But McAllister is enjoying blowing up the naiveté.

"These aren't the conventional lessons, Duncan. This isn't something that your teachers will tell you, or your dad, or anyone but those dismissed as loony conspiracy theorists. But just think about it for a minute, because not all conspiracy theorists are created equal. What happens when something is illegal, and will always be demanded and, thus, will always be supplied? Its value is maximized. It's Economics 101. Because there's a far greater risk involved in supplying it, that supply can be controlled, with a risk that's justifiable because there's *exponentially* more money to be made from that supply. It's profit maximization, you see? By making it illegal, by putting supply in the hands of those willing to make themselves criminals to supply it, profit skyrockets."

"I see…"

The beads of sweat on McAllister's reddened brow grow, and he loosens his tie. He continues his sermon, albeit sweating and labored, the train looking like it'll derail.

"Yes, if made legal, or at least decriminalized, more people *might* be tempted to use those drugs, but the environment in which they'd be used would be *far* safer, as the removal of the criminal element removes the danger of dealing with criminals. And the health dangers involved in those consumers hiding and illegally using those substances, instead of being monitored, taxed, protected and educated, would be *drastically* curtailed."

"Interesting..." But he's struggling to listen. Not only is Mr. McAllister's sweating becoming profuse, but the mention of the increased risk of illegal substance use has his mind jumping to that horrible scene at the hospital, and to Dan's insinuation that Caroline was killed for selling drugs on a far bigger drug-dealer's turf.

"*Disturbing*, Duncan. Disturbing. And many of those plugged into the national and international power centers are well aware of this. So, do you think they just sit back and let the crooks make all of the money off of all of these... *activities*? Do you think those in power, taking orders from their campaign financiers, just sit back and leave the mightiest sword of globalization, the U.S. Military and all its profiteering weapons suppliers, in its sheath in all of this? Of course not! Do you think that controlling the supply of the *massively* profitable drug market is unrelated to our military history in Afghanistan, South-East Asia and Central and Southern America, the global centers of narco-production? Of course not! I wish I could wake the American people up to this fact, Duncan, I really do, but I wouldn't last in office past my first speech. I'd be defunded, or laughed off the stage, or killed outright."

"That's not exactly how those military campaigns were taught in U.S. History class…"

"Nope. No way. You think the powers I speak of would allow that? And the biggest front in all of this is the fake War on Drugs itself. That false sham of a war exists for the same reason the War on Terror exists: it's a façade

     The House on Apple Blossom Lane

built to trick the masses into thinking the government and the wealthy and powerful that control it care about things that they really don't; that they care about drug addiction and all the social fallout and communities in ruin and disrepair, or, when it comes to the War on Terror, that they're, you know, trying to free people from dictators and backwards belief systems and install freedom and democracy. All the while they're picking the new so-called elected leaders and plugging their own corporate interests in the best positions to profit, very often propped up by even *more* diabolical dictators."

Duncan says nothing. He just stares at McAllister. He's standing now, pacing behind his desk while offloading his thoughts. Wobbling a bit, he abruptly stops and places both hands on his desk. He's gone from his purging soliloquy to looking like he could fall onto his desk at any moment. Duncan thinks of what he's heard in the past about these important men living with so much stress that a quarter of them keel-over from heart attacks before they reach the age of fifty.

"It's another concealed fact, Duncan, because people are naïve, but the truth is that it's in the very psychological nature of wealth and power possession to conspire for more of it..." He's breathing heavily, the words ejected with effort. "The truth is that all the major players are conspiring all the time, we just don't call it conspiring or plotting when it looks like it's aboveboard business or politics as usual. But what appears aboveboard often dips belowboard. In fact, it can be very hard to tell the difference between the two. Which is why people like your father exist, I hate to say... And if you think those connected to the political power centers are immune to the psychology of power, to motive, means and opportunity, and that they let opportunities pass them up simply because they're so-called representatives of the people and stand upon moral high ground, then you're a fool. In fact, it's much the opposite. *Because* they're informed and in positions of power, *because* they influence budgets operating in the billions or trillions and see all the private opportunities connected to political operations, because they represent the immensely lucrative grey area set between the public and private sectors, that makes them *more* likely to conspire, not less."

"You should write a book..."

"No, it would never make it to print. Because it isn't truth and morality that writes the story, Duncan. And, sadly, it's all the same story, with different financial opportunities involved. With one hand they condemn and fight it, keeping profit margins high and wiping-out competitors, all while holding the other hand out of sight, like shady magicians manipulating misdirection, reaching as deep into the till as they can, taking the biggest possible cut. Only a strict minority of those of us in the know have the strength to fight this truth, and it doesn't make us popular, let me tell you, Duncan. I do what I can... but we all have to survive, my boy."

"So, what are you saying, that the people that are a part of the organization supposedly helping your son, and my friends, is, what, a part of this somehow?"

"There's nothing specific that I can tell you, Duncan. I can only tell you generally that, with so much money to be made, a *lot* gets invested in making sure that the hand that gets held out in front is the hand that gets seen by most. Read your Machiavelli. That's Politics 101. A lot goes into making things appear precisely the opposite of the way things are. Because if the public were to have anything *close* to an accurate sense of what the other hand is doing, if the monster was unmasked and his deception revealed, well, let's just say the fallout would be beyond words. The lost profits would be beyond counting, as would the prison time."

"But, Mr. McAllister, I need to know what to do…"

He's seated now. Duncan is starting to worry that he should do something. It's like he's slowly losing his ability to remain upright.

"There's really not a lot that you *can* do, Duncan. Because there's no part of the apparatus that you can really interrupt. Even guys like me that try to throw a wrench in the local machinery and grind the gears that we can reach know that there's no touching the big machine; the one whose pullies stretch across the nation, and then across the world. Break one cog, another cog comes in to fill it. Now, I try, trust me, I do. I can do my best to keep my own constituents as safe as possible. And I sure as hell am not just going to sit back and let their own tax dollars support the trafficking."

Duncan recalls the fact that Washington State was listed along with several other government entities and the pharmaceutical companies as those supporting Trauma Research and Counseling. 'How do the strings connect?'

Donald McAllister hits a button on his black corded phone. "Lisa, will you bring me some water, please?"

"Of course, sir," intones back.

"Now, all that said, Duncan, I must reiterate that I don't want my sons involved in any of this. I don't want *any* of you kids involved, actually. Anything coming anywhere close to that world is *far* too dangerous, which I'm guessing that your father has already told you. And which is why you're here, because you're dipping your toes into a fiery lake that's going to burn you alive." As he says this his affect becomes sorrowful. Duncan thinks he's about to tear up. He briefly turns his head, and when he turns back he's the politician again, albeit one appearing on the verge of a myocardial infarction.

"When I realized where Dan would be living, I just wanted to warn him about staying away from trouble. The rest of it he must've inferred, and he's probably exaggerating or misreading what he thinks he's experienced. And I never gave him such a mission, and you're to cease any involvement immediately, okay?"

"Yes, sir."

"Everything that you've been hinting at… I can't go into specifics, but suffice it to say that there's already an investigation under way, and that you interjecting yourself into the situation will only mean you'll be getting in our way, and putting yourself in jeopardy."

A silence passes between them. Images of recent events battle in Duncan's brain, their proper placement eluding him.

"If you really want to help, Duncan, you can encourage Dan to steer clear of it all. You can try to dissuade him from following anything that sounds delusional. I don't want to betray his trust, so I won't say too much, but you should know that not everything that my son says is based in reality... And where it comes to *your* father, I don't know how much he knows, but all you can do is try to encourage him to come forward and work with the authorities. We can make your family safe. Tell him that I would more than welcome his cooperation. I can put him in touch with the right people. Coming forward and getting him some protection is the best case scenario for him. And you. And if he's involved in anything illegal already, working with us is the only way to avoid prison. Now, would you mind asking my secretary to come in?"

The last thing he hears while exiting is McAllister's secretary concernedly inquiring: "Should I call for a doctor, sir?"

On the way back to his car, Duncan feels faint himself. All the stress and thinking, the mental and physical exhaustion, are taking their toll. 'I don't think I can do this. But I have to. I have to find some way to expose the truth... to throw it into the full light of day such that it can't be denied, and the authorities will be *forced* to act, regardless of the interests of any of these... higher-ups.'

Walking through the large parking lot, he unlocks and is a few strides from his Prius when a grey sedan comes in from the side directly in front of him and slams on the breaks. *Its Marie*. She smiles through the windshield and drops her driver's side window, leaning her head out.

"Hello, Duncan."

"Marie! What are you doing here?"

"I need to talk to you, Duncan. Get in."

"Good, I could really use your help."

He starts to pass his Prius to get into Marie's car, a grey sedan that he's never seen before, when another, larger vehicle comes screeching in from back and behind him, in the next row over in the lot.

"Shit!," Marie screams. "Get down, Duncan!"

Duncan drops down to the pavement beside his car as Marie reaches somewhere down below and grabs a pistol, but just as she raises it so that Duncan can see it, shots are fired from behind him. The bullets ricochet all around him, some hitting his Prius and many more slamming into the side of Marie's car. Covering his ears, he crouches and crawls towards cover behind another vehicle. Glancing up at Marie, he sees her duck down and her car accelerate. In an instant her sedan is out of eyeshot. Suddenly an immense figure comes in from the opposite direction, blocking the sun. It's Mr. Romero. He has something in his hand. It looks like a yellow stun gun.

Adrenaline fires, and Duncan's on his feet sprinting away, weaving his way between parked cars. Turning around, he sees Romero with his gun raised, pointed right at him. Instinctively Duncan ducks, then continues sprinting away in a serpentine pattern, between cars, trying to be unpredictable, expecting to be hit by something at any moment. But it doesn't happen. After snaking through a few more rows, thinking he hears footsteps behind him, he catches sight of the main street leading into the lot and makes a break for it, feeling like being in public might afford him some protection.

Crashing through a large, thorny shrub that slashes at his face and arms, he comes near to falling into the busy street in front of the capitol. A car slams on its breaks and honks angrily as Duncan finds his balance just in time to keep from crashing into it. Turning his head around, there's no sign of Romero. He turns to run down the street in what looks like the most populated direction, hearing sirens somewhere behind him. Running for blocks, he pauses only momentarily at intersections, crossing a few streets without the walk signal activated, doing anything he can to put distance between himself and the menace behind him. Lungs burning, chest heaving, he spots a convenience market and darts inside, crashing into a stand of chips and beef jerky, almost knocking it over, startling a couple of customers.

Running towards the back of the store, Duncan doesn't see the yellow "Wet Floor" sign on the ground just prior to the wall of cold drinks. Slipping, he spills forward and slams his head and shoulder into one of the glass doors, cracking the pane and causing a woman nearby to shriek. The cashier at the counter runs over to assess the situation as Duncan, dazed, attempts to get to his feet, but he's unsuccessful, and slumps back to the floor, his back to the cracked door. Running back to the front counter, the cashier calls the police. Duncan can just comprehend the gist of the report: a young man out of control; property damage; probably on drugs.

Something wet drips down his face. Duncan reaches up and touches the right side of his head, feeling the gash. A thin stream of blood trickles through his hair down the side of his face. Soon the cashier approaches him again, cautiously, as if curious about him but keeping his distance from a potentially dangerous animal. A moment later, and he seems to decide that Duncan is harmless.

"Are you okay, sir?," he asks Duncan, slowly approaching. He's a young Asian kid, maybe a few years older than Duncan, with gold jewelry and a tattoo of a dragon on the left side of his neck, just poking out of his shirt.

"Yea. I'm okay... I think."

"The police are on their way. To... *help you*."

'Shit. Is that bad?,' he wonders. 'I don't even know anymore.' He suddenly gets the urge to tell the kid everything. Maybe it'll offload some of the strain he's carrying around in his body and brain. But he doesn't. Instead, he simply says: "He was trying to kill me."

A squad car soon arrives. The first officer to enter has his gun drawn, as if expecting to meet with an armed hostile. Instead he finds Duncan, out of it, leaning against the cracked glass door. The officer and his partner holster their weapons and start to question him.

"This doesn't have anything to do with the shooting in the Capitol Center parking lot, does it?" He almost tells them the truth, then thinks: 'It'll take more than a police report with local law enforcement to take these guys down. If the FBI is getting stalled, what are city cops going to do? It'll only make matters worse.'

The police don't cuff him, but insist upon taking him in.

"We're going to need to take an official statement from you, Duncan, since property damage was involved."

On the way to the station he gives the police his father's phone number. When they arrive at the station, the officers are told by their Sargent to "Wait for his father to arrive. He's a lawyer, and insists on being present if we're going to question his son." Under his voice he adds: "He sounds like a cocky fucker, so be careful."

Seated beside one of the officer's desks, Duncan ruminates on what to report. Again, he vacillates between honesty and deception. He wants so badly for everything to be over, even though he couldn't be more doubtful of the officer's capacity to end things in a manner that would benefit everyone involved; himself, his father, Marie, and poor Dan, caught between both sides of a fast-closing vice.

Upon arrival, Jonathan Mills insists upon speaking with his "client" in private before a statement is made, but Duncan refuses.

"No, Dad, I'm just going to tell them what happened."

His father, wide-eyed, speaks up to protest, but Duncan proceeds:

"A guy pulled a knife on me a few blocks from the convenience store. I think he wanted to rob me. So I ran. I thought the store might have a back way out so I could evade the guy, but I didn't see the slippery floor sign, and I slipped and fell. That's pretty much it."

 The House on Apple Blossom Lane

Duncan can feel his father's relief as he says this, his entire demeanor changing. The officers seem incredulous, and clearly suspect there's more going on, what with their hushed voice conferrals with their Sergeant and what appears to be an in-house lawyer in the time between his own arrival at the station and that of his father's. "You sure this has nothing to do with the shooting in the parking lot of the Capitol Center, son?"

"He just told you what happened," Jonathan Mills intercedes. "Now, if no criminal charges are being filed, I suggest you let my client go."

Duncan makes a statement as to the physical features of his phantom accoster, and gives vague details as to the location of the fictitious assault. He describes a tall bulky white guy with cold blue eyes and dark, slicked-back hair, thinking of Mr. Romero and Donald McAllister as he says it, as if he's describing their composite. Jonathan Mills gives the police his information, "so that I can pay for any damages," and soon they're on their way home.

Only, they *aren't* headed home. In his hazy, exhausted state, and with darkness fast descending, it takes Duncan longer than it would otherwise to realize that they're headed into the *city*, not the suburbs. Soon, the distant sound of jet engines can be heard. *The airport.*

"I know that you went to see Donald McAllister," his father says quietly. "That was really, really stupid, Duncan. That may've been the last straw. I don't know what happened in that parking lot, and I don't think that I want to know. But Mr. Carpenter knows it too. Knows more than I do, most likely. He called me. He told me there was some trouble there, and that Mr. Romero had to intervene to keep one of McAllister's people from kidnapping or killing you. You're lucky they *didn't* kill you. He says that you may've compromised all of us."

Duncan thinks of telling him about Marie; about the firefight; about the fact that she was probably there to save him. But he doesn't understand it, and he's still in a slight state of shock, his body trembling. His father probably wouldn't believe it anyway. He'd say he was lying to avoid responsibility. In fact, his father tragically seems unable to even entertain the *possibility* of doing anything beyond following Carpenter's orders.

"Give me your keys," Jonathan Mills commands his youngest son. His voice is low, but firm, and filled with equal measures of defeat and exhaustion. 'He's acting like we're already dead.' As Duncan reluctantly hands over his keys, his father adds: "I'll try to retrieve your car from the lot, if it's still there. Hopefully whatever happened wasn't caught on tape. If it was, I may not be able to prevent the authorities from tracking you down out east and bringing you back. But for now, there's only one thing left for me to do with you, and that's get you as far away as I can from this slow-moving trainwreck."

Normally he'd protest. 'This isn't over,' he thinks. But he doesn't say anything. He decides that it isn't worth the effort. He needs to save all the energy and strength that he has left for what lies ahead. His father, too, falls silent. Both he and his boy are beyond depleted.

Pulling into Seattle International Airport, Jonathan Mills removes a large suitcase of his son's from the trunk of his white Chrysler 300. As they head through the entrance and to the service desks, scarcely a word is uttered between them. Jonathan buys his son a first class ticket to New Haven, Connecticut, keeping an eye on him the entire time, as if afraid his stubborn, reckless son may bolt at any moment. But Duncan hasn't the energy to overcome the two men corralling him.

His father secures special permission to accompany his son, along with a security officer, through security and to the departure gate, citing some legal justification that Duncan can't hear. Outside the gate, his father and the security guard seated on either side of him, Duncan dozes off in the forty minutes between the time he arrives at the gate and the arrival of his flight, departing at 7:05 PM. His father's pat on the shoulder wakes him up. The security guard departed while he slept.

As a first class passenger, Duncan is seated near the outset of the boarding process. He waits patiently for the plane to fill, watching the door the entire time. Finally, it's apparent that no more passengers are going to be boarding. The head stewardess makes a move for the door, preparing to secure it. Duncan stands and makes his move.

"Excuse me, ma'am, but I need to get off."

"We're about to depart, young man, please return to your seat."

"I'm sorry, but I just realized that I forgot my medication. There's no way that I can fly all the way to the East Coast without it. It's for a severe liver disease. I could die without it."

The stewardess looks at her colleague, who gives her a nod of assent, and a minute later Duncan is walking briskly back up the gangway. He proceeds up the final length with caution. Poking his head out, he looks at where his father had been seated when he entered the gangway, when he'd been playing it cool, pretending not to be hyperaware of his position. He's not there. Leaning out further, he glances to his left, nothing; to his right, and there he is. His father is watching the plane out the window. The entry to the gangway has been roped-off, and the only remaining gate attendant is conversing with a customer. Watching his dad, Duncan ducks under the rope and moves

　　The House on Apple Blossom Lane

swiftly out of sight in the opposite direction, his heart heavy. He can't stand to betray or deceive his father. But running away to some false sense of safety to await his father's doom would be even worse. Ten minutes later and his Uber driver has arrived to pick him up at the domestic terminal entrance.

"Where to?"

"6160 Apple Blossom Lane."

Chapter 9

It's nearing dusk when Duncan once again approaches 6160 Apple Blossom Lane. As far as he can tell, there's no one in the street keeping watch. No sign of the seemingly omnipresent Mr. Romero. And no sign of life at TRACE, other than the faint electronic glow of its computers behind the closed blinds.

As he approaches the front door of 6160, he can hear conversation inside. The house is well lit. It sounds like everyone is home. But Duncan stops upon seeing the large laminated sign red-taped across the door:

"Washington Public Safety Notice: This house is under quarantine. No entry of non-residents permitted without the express written consent of the Washington Department of Public Health, Olympia, WA."

Duncan pauses, wondering at the level of danger, but quickly comes to the conclusion that he's already been inoculated. 'What my dad gave me *has* to be for this. Saying that it wasn't was just another one of his lies.'

Suddenly feeling exposed on the street, and paranoid that someone *could* be watching, he knocks softly. Seconds later the locks are undone, and Dan swings the door open.

"Duncan! I didn't expect to see you again, honestly."

"What do you mean?"

Dan sticks his head out the door, looks up and down the street and across the street at TRACE, then wraps his arm around Duncan and pulls him inside. 'Is it paranoia if you're *right*?,' Duncan wonders.

"Well, I just didn't think the powers that be would allow you to keep playing this game, that's all," Dan responds. "But they must have their reasons… they must *want* you here for some reason," he adds. As he says it his eyes exhibit fear and suspicion, and he looks Duncan up and down, as if he may be inviting an enemy into his base.

"I'm on your side, Dan, I swear."

This seems to placate Dan a bit, who keeps eyeing Duncan with suspicion, though a bit less anxiously. "I hope so…" Dan says. "Well, I suppose if you have the balls to cross the quarantine, you must be motivated by something more than the need to spy on us."

"Luckily TRAC has worked out some sort of deal with the college," Mia speaks up, having entered the foyer, "and we've been given permission to finish out the semester here, in quarantine. Hello Duncan, it's good to see you again. Why are you here?"

"I…" Duncan starts, but glancing at Dan, who gives him a slight head shake 'no,' he decides not to divulge too much. "I just needed to talk to Dan about something…"

Mia eyes the two of them suspiciously, then says: "Well, *okay*… Hopefully this isn't more of that 'TRACE is a super villain organization thing of yours, sweetie,'" she says to Dan. "We really can't afford more of that, not if we're going to get through this semester, especially considering that *they're* the ones allowing us to do so. Duncan, I hope you're not encouraging that… *fantasy*."

"No, I…"

"Can you just give us a few minutes, please, Mia? We'll be in shortly."

"Fine," she says with irritation before returning to the living room.

Dan leads Duncan around the other side of the first story of the home, towards the kitchen in the back of the house. "So, what's up?," he asks Duncan. "I haven't seen you since we found out about Caroline. And I'm really, *really* sorry about Samantha, Duncan. It looked like the two of you were close. Or going to be... Personally, I think she was collateral damage from TRACE targeting Caroline for selling drugs out of their house."

"I think you might be right, honestly. I mean, the whole thing sounds crazy... shit, sorry, probably a poor choice in words."

"It's okay. It *is* crazy. But you have no idea how glad I am that you think that it might be possible. I was starting to feel like my ideas were just delusions..."

"I spoke with your father. He told me that he never wanted you involved in any of this. He said that you misunderstood him."

"Of course he did."

"But I don't think that matters now. Because he seems certain that this group that's helping you, TRAC, is some sort of narcotics trafficking front, just like you said. And, at this point, I need some evidence. Something that I can take to the authorities as proof; something that I can leverage for the benefit of all of us. Because if we can't get something... *definitive*... something that'll put a stop to all of this... something we can show the cops or the FBI that *proves* these guys are drug runners, then I don't think we're getting out of this. I can feel the walls closing in, and I know you can too. And I know you and Michael thought my dad was the bad guy in all of this, but I think he's a victim too. And they're going to kill him, I know it, unless I find some way to get him out of this, fast."

"You might be right... I only know that your dad was involved from talking to my own."

"We need to get him out, Dan. I already lost my mother. She might've been killed by the TRAC people, for all I know. But unless we have proof we can use to make some sort of deal…"

"How are we going to find proof of anything? Especially considering this quarantine…"

"I don't know how, but we have to find a way. We have to look for *how* they're using this Trauma Research and Counseling thing to cover-up their drug smuggling, if that's what's really going on."

"The trucks," Dan says softly, as though having an epiphany.

"What trucks?"

"There was this one night not too long ago… I was studying in the little library they have in the TRAC building on campus, working on this boring assignment about classifying the differences between all the personality disorders and how they're developed… Anyway, I fell asleep. And when I woke up it was late. Like 9 pm. I heard something down the hallway. It was Professor Gilbert, I think. I'm taking one of his classes right now: on Reprogramming Traumatic Memories."

"I know, I saw the assignment sheet… before it disappeared when we were asleep. I remember his name."

"Right… the whole reenactment thing you said we did…"

"Yes… I still can't believe you don't remember that, Dan."

"I believe you. My head is messed up, Duncan. Anyway… I heard the professor talking to someone, then go downstairs. And I grabbed all my stuff and went downstairs and was going to tell him goodbye, you know, and laugh about how I'd fallen asleep… but when I spotted him out the doorway I got spooked, because he was talking to these two security guards and my counselor, Charlie Kaufman, the one Greta calls Sir Charles... you remember him, don't you?"

"Yes, I remember him. He was there that first night I came here... I have the peculiar sense that he violated me somehow, but of course I have no proof... not even a clear memory of *how* he violated me. I just have this vague sense that he made me do something that I didn't want to do..."

"Right... sorry, I don't remember that either..." He shakes his head at this ongoing admission of memory loss, and appears as though he may break down and start crying, but he takes a deep breath and continues:

"So he was there talking to Professor Gilbert about something in a low voice... something made me feel very uncomfortable about it, to the degree that I felt like approaching them might be dangerous. Gilbert kept repeating the words 'experiment, dosage and TRACE residents...' I thought that, maybe Charlie was getting the professor's advice on some sort of treatment or something. I didn't think that they worked together directly until then, and I kind of forgot about it until you said we needed proof just now..."

Dan fades out, then stares off, blankly, drifting away.

"Yes, and, so, what does that incident have to do with getting proof, Dan?"

"Right... well, they walked over and opened this gate with the security guards and all these vehicles drove into the area near the Pharmacological Sciences building across the way... it was weird how many... there were two medium-sized transport trucks, one with TRAC's logo on the side of it and one from the pharmaceutical company that works with us... what is it..? BridleChem. But there were also these two other regular trucks that pulled up… and these guys jumped out of them… these really sketchy looking dudes… they made the hairs stand up on the back of my neck, I remember now… they made me feel like I did in Afghanistan, like I was looking at an enemy combatant… They were moving a bunch of boxes between the trucks. I got really paranoid watching, even from a distance, so I backed off and walked away… I don't think anyone saw me. Somehow the whole incident slipped my mind until now…"

"So, what, you think they were moving drugs, and not just pharmaceutical drugs?"

"Maybe… I mean, *now* I think so… If there was some way to find out… maybe we could get this evidence of yours. If I can sneak back into that area, I can try to find a way to take a closer look this time."

"It sounds risky, Dan."

The House on Apple Blossom Lane

"You said yourself the walls are closing in. I figure it's the best chance we have. I can try to film it from afar. Get some of it on tape, and maybe some of their faces. What other choice do we have?"

"Ok... Then we'll divide and conquer. You look for these trucks, and I'll try to find some other proof. I might be able to find something in my dad's office at home, or maybe I can find an excuse to get into the TRACE office and, like, read some files or install some sort of camera or listening device. I know that probably sounds silly, but those things are *so* small and cheap and easy to hide these days... I saw this investigative report a week ago about how it's become easier than ever for stalkers to install these devices and keep track of their victims. Maybe I can turn the tables on them; the stalked becoming the stalker. If I can just install something..."

"You know, now that you say that, I'm pretty sure that Mia has something like that in her room. She bought this pair of small cameras and a microphone to install in her room last month when she was paranoid that someone was sneaking into her room while she was at class. And later we were laughing about it, and decided to keep them running for... our own purposes," he adds with a snort. "I'll bet that I could convince her to at least give you the mini microphone thing."

"Good, that would be..."

"Guys, c'mon, *please*," Mia pleads from the living room. "If we're going to do this virtual reality 'A Walk in the Park' assignment in time to fill out the questionnaire tonight, Dan, then we have to get it started soon."

"She's right... I have to maintain appearances," Dan says. "I doubt I'll actually be able to get through the semester, but if I don't try they'll have even more of a reason to suspect me of something..."

Duncan drops his head. "I'm really sorry about all this, Dan. It was never my intention…"

"It's not your fault, Duncan… But, hey, since you're here and breaking the quarantine with us, maybe you'd like to try this new thing with us," he adds while walking into the living room.

"What is it?"

In the living room George, Greta and Mia are wearing what look like large black motorcycle helmets with fancy visors. There's a small electronic box on the table that looks like a small wireless router.

"It's like the old COVID days that I *thought* were behind us," Greta speaks up, "when everyone tried to carry on everything virtually. We're back to that, I suppose. It's very unfortunate in a way, but I bet it's fun at least."

"Yea, at least TRAC has some cool toys for us to play with during our mystery COVID strain quarantine," George offers.

"And how do we know we can *trust* these toys?," Duncan whispers to Dan. "You didn't see what I saw the last time…"

Dan hesitates. Mia walks over and grabs him by the hand, drawing him over to the couch, before placing one of the helmets on him.

"It's just a school assignment," she assures them. "Please, Duncan, my boyfriend is worrisome enough without you breathing oxygen onto his fires. Besides, none of us remember that action movie reenactment thing you were talking about before. We're all fine."

"Yea, but…"

"Look, Duncan, you're welcome to stay," Mia continues, "but we have this so-called 'virtual nature immersion therapy' assignment to complete, and it's getting late. Care to join us? It might be cool. It's a virtual visitation of the state park at the end of the lane."

There's one more headset. Like it was set there for him on purpose, just in case he were to show up. The thought of it being a trap feels suffocating.

"No, I'm fine. May I borrow your cameras? And the microphone? The stuff that Dan was talking about."

With a huff, Mia begrudgingly runs upstairs and retrieves two small cameras and an even smaller microphone from her bedroom and hurries through an explanation of how to install and use it.

"I'll get to that... *other* thing soon," Dan says meekly as Duncan heads for the door.

"What other thing, Dan?" Mia is ready to pounce on them both, her face reddening.

"Nothing, love." He hurries into the living room and dutifully takes his seat on the couch, Mia on his left, Greta and George on his right.

Standing in the foyer, reaching for the door handle, Duncan is hesitant to leave. He looks back into the living room, remembering the last time he observed the group in the same position. A powerful urge to run over, grab the fancy headsets and spike them into the ground, shattering them into pieces before stomping all over their remnants, comes over him. But he does nothing, feeling trapped by catch-22 circumstances.

All of their headsets are secured, with Mia leading the group. She says: "Everyone ready?" They all give their verbal assent, Dan rather reluctantly. Mia pushes a large green button on the electronic box on the table. The box and their headsets immediately begin to emit soft, blue light, and seconds later the comments begin.

"Whoa…" the group utters in unison.

Duncan, holding the small cameras and microphone in one arm awkwardly, as though cradling a child, cords dangling, reaches with the other arm to open the front door when a thought occurs to him; a thought triggered by glancing at the cameras that he's holding.

'How could I be so stupid? I came in through the front door! We *looked* to see if they were watching, but if I'm going to try to watch them they *must* be watching me! They must know I'm here already!' He thinks of sleep, and his inability to think clearly under duress. 'I'll have a better chance of pulling this off if I at least *try* to remain undetected. I can sleep later, when we're all safe.'

Moving through the living room, Duncan is again unsettled by the sense that the reality in which the residents currently reside makes them oblivious to their actual surroundings. 'So vulnerable,' he thinks, walking feet from their faces without the slightest reaction. 'Like caged animals that don't even know they're in a cage.'

Their oohs and aahs continue unabated. Apparently they're in a virtual forest, and spellbound by its realism. Greta is mesmerized by a flower. Mia thinks she can smell something pleasant in the air. George giggles like a child, at what, exactly, Duncan can only wonder. Only Dan remains silent, an odd scowl on his face. Making his way to the back door, Duncan turns around in concern, wondering if he should ask Dan what's wrong, but knows that he can't without evoking Mia's wrath. Looking out the sliding glass door into the backyard, making sure the coast is clear, he's reaching for the handle when he hears Dan speak up.

"I'm going to make us a campfire. It'll be dark soon," he says flatly.

"What do you mean?," Greta incredulously asks. Her head points up as she says: "It looks like it's the middle of the day to me."

Pulling a lighter from his pocket, Dan sparks it and, reaching out and grabbing the stack of assignment papers in front of him, he lights them on fire and drops them into the middle of the wooden table. Freezing, remembering the violence of the last 'reenactment,' Duncan turns to launch himself towards the group when Dan calmly says: "A bear." The words are spoken like someone trying to maintain their cool in the face of danger. This further locks Duncan in place. He isn't sure why. Fear? Morbid curiosity? "A bear," Dan repeats with agitation. Then, with increasing volume and fear fast turning into outright terror: "A bear. A bear! A BEAR!!"

"Where? What are you talking about Dan?,"
Mia asks, she and Greta and George looking
all around them.

Transfixed, Duncan's attention is suddenly
caught by something moving outside.
Looking, he sees a drone out the window,
only a few feet from the glass. It appears to
be pointed right at him. *Then the sound.*
Almost imperceptible at first, and emitted
from an unknown source, or *sources*, within
the house, it's a high-pitched buzzing sound.
Dropping the equipment on the kitchen floor,
Duncan's first impulse is to move towards
Dan and yank the headset off of him, but the
sound suddenly increases in pitch and
volume, to the point where he involuntarily
drops to his knees. Vision blurring, feeling like
he's going to pass out, it takes all of his
strength to yank open the door and crawl
out. He's just able to push the sliding glass
door closed with his foot and avoid losing
consciousness, the drone buzzing around his
head the entire time, changing positions as

　　　The House on Apple Blossom Lane

though it's being directed by someone that wants to capture every angle.

In his agony, all Duncan can think of is escaping the scene. Looking to his right towards the granny unit, he sees Charlie Kaufman, Dan's counselor, the one that Mia had called 'Sir Charles,' standing just outside the door, on his cellphone. Wide-eyed, he's looking at Duncan and talking to someone. Suddenly Duncan is overcome by rage, and Charlie is the target; the one responsible for all of it. Caroline and Samantha. Dan. His father. Even his dead mother. On his feet, he charges Charlie as Charlie pulls a card from his pocket and nervously fumbles at the keypad entry into the small structure.

"It's the lawyer's kid," Kaufman shouts. "Campfire has been initiated, but…"

Hurriedly swiping his card and typing in a code into the keypad to the right of the metal door, Charlie steps through and is turning around to shut the door when Duncan launches himself through the opening, crashing into him. He's entered some sort of control room, with a tech monitoring a series of screens to his left. But Duncan barely notices. In a fit of pure rage he's slamming Charlie's face into the metal floor until he stops moving. Now lying on the ground, looking around him, Duncan locks eyes with the tech, a middle-aged man with thick black glasses and closely-cropped grey hair.

The tech is standing up with his back up against the far wall, at the end of a large desk stacked with monitors, a look of shock upon his face. And for good reason. Duncan's ire unabated, he looks around to find something to bash his new target with, settling on a black metal plate, a piece of a large black filing cabinet being assembled beside Charlie's unconscious body. For a moment he wonders if he's killed him, his head badly bleeding. But his compassion fast disappears as he finally clearly recalls being commanded

　　The House on Apple Blossom Lane

to run home naked before, and the glee on Charlie's face as he issued the command. The fact that Duncan wasn't able to refuse the absurd order now coalesces into rage.

Seizing the black metal plate for the filing cabinet under-construction, he turns back around, the tech fleeing through the open door just in time to avoid being hacked at. A moment later the drone buzzes through the same opening. In one motion Duncan stands and swings ferociously at the hovering contraption with the piece of the metal file drawer, knocking it into the monitor on the far left side of the desk. It falls to the floor. The camera on the drone whirls around, like the eye of someone about to lose consciousness, focusing on him a moment before he brings the sharp edge of the plate down upon it as hard as he can, once, twice, three times knifing it with the piece of metal, shattering it into pieces, feeling the fury triumphantly release from his body. Then, chest heaving, Duncan drops his repurposed weapon and starts examining the space.

Twelve small monitors are stacked into two neat rows on the desk in front of where the tech had been seated. On the walls behind the seat in the small unit, the entire space measuring no more than ten by twenty feet, it looks like a science lab. Glass containers filled with fluids of various colors sit beside boxes of syringes and masks, an odd assortment of equipment stacked beside them. The largest machine by far, taking up half of the space opposite the desk, says "ENVIRONMENTAL CONTROL AEROSOL SYSTEM" across the top of it in big, bold, capital letters, with six circular ports spread evenly across the center of the machine and the words "Input 1," "Input 2" etc. stamped into metallic tags above them.

All the input ports are empty except for the first one, the far left port, which holds a large cylindrical glass canister that's uniformly misted within with a bright pink fluid that reminds Duncan of the color of Pepto Bismol. Each port appears to be connected to a pipe dropping from the bottom of the machine into the ground, disappearing from sight. It hums softly, its only display, a small six by six inch screen, repeatedly blinking with the words "NO. 1 COMPLETE." Numerous other cylinders are set beside the machine, some empty, some filled with liquids of various colors, mostly in hues of blue and red.

Turning around, Duncan's borderline OCD fastidiousness grips him, as the first thing he notices is that a manilla envelope on the desk, set to the left of the keyboard, is about to be ruined. Already streaked with brown coffee stains, the corner of the envelope is tucked under a miniature coffee machine, and it's soon to absorb the rest of the coffee flowing its direction from the nearby mug the tech knocked over. Picking it up, the envelope has been signed by his father, a signature he's seen countless times throughout his youth, legal papers having been omnipresent at home growing up. "On TRAC 2020: Strategic Summary" is printed in his father's handwriting just above where he's signed it. There's no time to open it or read its contents now, so he quickly folds and stuffs it into his pants pocket as his eyes leap to the horror unfolding on the monitors in front of him.

Duncan leans over the desk holding the two rows of six monitors each, realizing he's looking into 6160 from various perspectives. "Emergency Lockdown... Operation Campfire" scrolls in repeating red at the bottom of every screen. One of them is fixed on the living room where, huddled in the corner near to the kitchen, Greta, George, Mia and Dan hug one another. He can hear them crying softly over the monitor, seemingly ignorant of the fact that they'll soon be consumed by flame.

'Fuck! They're not reacting! I have to save them!'

Stepping outside, night descending, he barely senses the presence of Mr. Carpenter's goon coming in from the left. Turning, he hears a click and, a moment later, something pierces him through his shirt, on his left shoulder. Then total agony. He falls to the grass, heaving with involuntary convulsions.

Darkness descends.

Chapter 10

Regaining consciousness, the first thing Duncan hears is:

"...family history of mental illness. He was an applicant for the TRAC program, for after he graduates from high school here in town. He found out that his mom was connected to our program and he blames us for her death, and for the death of his girlfriend. A student from his high school, Samantha. She contracted COVID here, unfortunately, and lost her fight with the virus. He convinced himself that we deliberately exposed her."

Duncan is sitting with his back against the wall of the secondary unit, handcuffed. The haze gradually lifting, he's listening to Charlie Kaufman make a report to a police officer. Several other officers survey the scene.

Behind Kaufman dozens of firefighters are working to put out the remains of 6160 Apple Blossom Lane. It's a smoldering char. Most of the home has collapsed. A thick wall of smoke rises from the debris. To his left, out in the street, nothing is getting through. It's packed with emergency personnel of every order, and three news vans. Student onlookers crowd the perimeter, filling Apple Blossom Lane in both directions.

"You killed them!," Duncan tries to scream, his voice faltering. The police officer turns and looks at him contemptuously. His eyes exhibit pure condescension. Duncan realizes that nothing that he says will matter. The cop has already decided that he's a criminal.

"We have footage, officer," Kaufman adds, not even looking Duncan's direction. He's holding an ice back up to his nose, grimacing and letting out the occasional groan. His face is a mess. "Footage of him entering through the front and coming out the back, and the home going up in flames seconds later."

"What about the footage of the virtual reality headsets? And Dan thinking he was starting a campfire?" This time the officer doesn't even bother looking at him.

An hour later, his endless protests and appeals falling upon deaf ears, Duncan is ushered from the back of the police cruiser into the local precinct. Held in confinement for over an hour, so exhausted he drifts into and out of consciousness a handful of times, he's eventually brought into an interview room, where he finds his father's partner Mr. Donovan seated across from two detectives. In a corner of the room, near the detectives, a television monitor on a black rolling cart is being remotely turned off by the detective sitting closest to it. In the two-second glimpse that Duncan catches, the screen had been broken into a dozen squares, seven of them black, smoke and flame filling the other five.

"Duncan, take a seat," Donovan orders.

Too tired to resist, he slumps into the black metal chair beside Donovan.

"These gentleman brought you in because they had good reason to believe that you started the fire that killed those four college kids."

"That's bullshit!"

"*However*," Donovan continues, "they've since been furnished with evidence that someone else started the fire. They also say that there's evidence that you killed the father of one of the victims, a Mr. McAllister, when you visited him in Olympia yesterday."

"What? I just wanted to talk to him about his sons, and Dad! Where's my dad..?"

"Your father is missing, Duncan. But Marie, your father's girlfriend, contacted me an hour ago and told me that you'd be needing my assistance here. She's outside. She'll be driving you home. They can't hold you for the murder of Mr. McAllister. Their evidence is circumstantial. However, in the spirit of goodwill I told them that you'd be willing to answer their questions."

Duncan tells the detectives almost everything. The rumors at school. Samantha and Caroline. The house on Apple Blossom Lane. He leaves out being shot at outside of McAllister's office. And when he begins to speak of his father's involvement, Donovan quickly quiets him.

"Only the house and McAllister, Duncan. Your father isn't under investigation."

Glad for the chance to vent, he keeps talking. But when Duncan mentions Carpenter and Romero, he freezes up, assuming Donovan will cut him off again in protection of the firm's clients. Yet, he doesn't interrupt, just stares at Duncan with an odd look on his face, nodding his head, encouraging him. Donovan seems afraid. But of what? 'He's not afraid of me ratting on *those* two?,' he thinks.

After detailing every event and suspicion that he has involving Carpenter and his granite-sculptured goon, Duncan assures the detectives that, if his father is missing, it could only be Carpenter and Romero that're to blame. They need to find him, and fast!

"We'll look into it, trust me," the lead detective assures him. "But, in the meantime, what about Mr. McAllister?"

"I told you, I was worried about my dad and his sons, especially Dan, and obviously for good reason!"

"Do you know anything about cyanide, Duncan?," the second detective cooly inquires.

"*No*. I mean, I've obviously heard of it. Who hasn't?"

"Do you know how to make it? How to extract it?"

"What? No! Of course not!"

"So it's just a coincidence that Mr. McAllister collapsed shortly after you left his office yesterday?"

"It has to be. I..." Suddenly an image from the visit flashes into his head. *The Fed Ex delivery woman.*

"*What*, Duncan?," the lead detective demands, reading Duncan's face.

Duncan instinctively senses that he shouldn't say anything about her. "Nothing," he replies after a long pause. "I was just trying to remember…"

Twenty minutes later Duncan exists the police station with Donovan. It's nearly ten p.m. Marie is waiting for them. Approaching them, she gives Donovan a little nod. Oddly, Donovan nods but says nothing. Giving Marie a wide berth, he says: "I hope your father turns up Duncan," and scurries past her into the parking lot.

"What's with him?," Duncan asks, eyeing Marie suspiciously.

"Wrong line of work," she says with a sly grin.

In the parking lot, his blue Ford Mustang idling, Michael McAllister watches as Mr. Donovan passes within ten feet of his vehicle and disappears behind him. But Michael's bloodshot, teary eyes never leave Duncan and Marie. Grinding his teeth and sporadically slamming his steering wheel with the palms of his hands, he watches his target as he enters the passenger side of Marie's black Escalade. Unbeknownst to him, she knows he's there. She drives home slowly enough to let him follow.

Cruising through the Seattle cityscape, the darkness intermittently interrupted by the glow of various white guiding lights and blinking neon advertisements, Duncan is clearly distressed. Appearing on the verge of tears, leaning his head against the glass, Marie can't help but think of him as an adopted son. She offers him mercy.

"Your father's fine, Duncan."

She says it with such certainty that, instead of relieving him, it frightens him. "What? How do you..."

"All I can tell you right now is that he stuck his neck *way* out there to get those detectives the video feed from inside the house to exculpate you. We had to get him out of the area. I'll take you to see him tomorrow."

"But…"

"Please don't ask me any more questions. I've told you all that I can."

The words are full of authority, as though a queen has been hiding within Marie all along, and has finally seen fit to grasp her scepter, and take command. It sends a chill up his spine. Turning his back to the door so as to put as much space between her and himself as possible, the words stick in his throat as he meekly asks:

"Who *are* you? Who is *we*?"

The blue in her eyes is emboldened by a steely glare his direction, as though her mien is made of ice. Her eyes seem so blue that he can see them in the dark. Duncan imagines that he's staring into a glacier. No, an *iceberg*. It's as though she's always been a mighty, capsizing block of ice, but, until now, the full force of her power, the magnitude of her persona, has been hiding beneath the calm surface of the water. It's finally on full display.

"Think of us as your father's... *silent partners*. As for me, I was here to establish and protect that partnership."

Driving the rest of the way home in silence, Duncan is a wreck. He's suddenly afraid of Marie, of this woman with whom he's shared a home for years and yet clearly had no clue about. He imagines endless scenarios as to who she is and everything his father has been wrapped up in without his knowing about it. But he's so tired that he can barely stand. So, upon entering their home through the garage he gives into her command to "eat something, then get to bed." A sedative is added to the leftover enchiladas that she reheats for him. She needs to make sure that he'll stay in his room through the night.

Twenty minutes later Duncan is snoring softly. Fully dressed, he'd spilled onto his bed like a pile of laundry. Marie stands over him, then circles his bed a few times, just to make sure. Satisfied, she wraps his bedspread around him and heads downstairs, then checks and reloads her weapon before sneaking out the back door, circling around the house and crossing the street. The low light of the new moon conceals her approach. Michael is parked at the curb a few houses down, watching their house. With one swift motion she's in his backseat, entering the Mustang via the back right door, squeezing into the tight space and holding a gun to the back of Michael's head before he can move.

He's been crying. He's lost everything. His father, his brother, even his girlfriend. When he feels the point of her gun press against the back right of his skull, he's almost glad. A part of him wants it all to be over, whoever this assailant is. But he wants vengeance even more. In his rearview he stares at the obscured figure.

"I know that you want revenge, Michael. And I know you blame Duncan and his father for what's happened to you. But you're wrong. They're not to blame. They're just pawns in a bigger chess match. Trust me. Because I'm like a... knight on that board. If you *really* want revenge I can help you get it. I can empower you to take out the king. Because I'm on the *inside* of that game. So I know what you don't. I know who's responsible, and how you can make sure that they're punished. But you'll have to follow my instructions *exactly*, or it won't work."

Head spinning, he can scarcely think. All he wants is an outlet for his rage. "Fine." It's all that he can manage. Minutes later Marie exits the vehicle, and Michael drives away.

Five hours later, in the wee hours of the morning, Marie steps past Charlie Kaufman and Professor Gilbert, both gagged and tied to one another, back against back, in the glass-walled office behind the receptionists' area of TRACE. The bodies of George, Greta, Mia and Dan were pulled from the smoking rubble across the street and sent to the morgue a few hours before, having been cleared from the remains of the house on Apple Blossom Lane. The area is free of law enforcement. For now.

Having used Jonathan Mills' security card and keycode to enter the building, she stuffs her pistol in the waistband in the back of her pants and uses the brief tutorial that Jonathan gave her to operate the three keyboards with attached computer monitors on the large desk. Cycling through over a hundred feeds from twenty-three cities across the country, everywhere that TRAC domestically operates, including adjacent

Pacific Northwest Healthcare College, she scans the video feeds whilst downloading the data from the three terminals onto a flash drive. Trucks from BridleChem, TRAC and Mission of Mexico, the no-cost health service that Darla Mills founded just before her death, move into and out of storage facilities attached to the twenty-three universities and several sites operated by BridleChem.

Completing the download, she loads up the laser printer to the right of the desk with extra paper before printing a selection of TRAC reports. The reports rapidly being printed, Kaufman and Gilbert's groans just audible over the soft hum of the machines, she picks up the black phone to the left of the desk and dials 911 before placing the receiver face-up beside the keypad. Removing the flash drive and stuffing it into her pocket, she purposefully triggers the security system on the computer. A silent alarm is tripped. But no images of her shall be captured. She's shot-out the half-dozen security cameras

The House on Apple Blossom Lane

onsite. As the reports overload the receiving paper tray and begin spilling onto the floor, she gives Kaufman a quick, winking glance before exiting.

Seven minutes and twenty-eight seconds later, Marie perched on a viewpoint knoll at the park half a mile from TRACE, the serene silence of dawn is pierced by the sirens of four police cruisers screaming onto the scene. She watches eight officers spill out of the cruisers and enter TRACE with their weapons drawn, then pulls her cell phone from her pocket and dials "#1." It rings once.

"Tell Mr. Arbusto that the roadblock has been cleared. I'll be bringing the hatchling to the nest tomorrow."

A few hours later, across town, Michael is parked across the street from the office of Mills and Associates. Just as Marie informed him, the black Lincoln Town Car pulls up to the curb out front. It's 7:15 am. Just like she said. They're there to meet Jonathan Mills. But he's AWOL.

Five minutes later, at exactly 7:20 am, there's an explosion at the top of the building, in the offices of Mills and Associates. Glass and debris rain down upon the Town Car. *That's his cue.* Time to pin them down.

Just as Mr. Romero puts the Town Car into drive and is about to floor it, the blue Mustang flies at them from the front and slams into the driver's side door, pinning and knocking Romero unconscious. Dazed, Carpenter spins out of the backseat and levels his pistol at Michael. Putting three bullets through the windshield, one of them strikes Michael in the forehead, killing him instantly. Turning to run, police swarm in.

Operating on an anonymous tip, they'd arrived a few minutes before, and had surrounded the scene. For a moment Carpenter considers shooting his way out, but thinks better of it. To screams from all sides commanding him to lower his weapon and get on the ground, the last thing he thinks before being cuffed is:

'They'll get me out of this. I know too much.'

Chapter 11

Waking up, Jonathan Mills' head is pounding. Wherever he is, he's never been here before. It's a well-appointed bedroom. Big, rustic-looking furniture. A gas fireplace with the mounted head of a bighorn sheep set over it. The bed feels plush. Rich. He's lying atop the bedspread, running his fingers over the embroidery of a Texas Flag.

A half-formed memory creeps up into his splitting skull, but it seems too odd to be real. The strangest feeling came over him while eating dinner with Marie the night before. He'd just placed a call to his oldest son, just to make sure he'd be there when Duncan landed, when a sensation came over him that he'd be hard-pressed to describe. Marie reached over, snatched his phone from him and turned it off. But instead of being angry, he was okay with it. He became giddy, almost euphoric, and quickly lost all sense of himself. Soon it was as if he was having one of those so-called 'out of body experiences.'

Marie shined the light from her own cell phone into his eyes, focusing on one eye and then the next, like you see the doctors do when they're checking pupillary responses. After that she grabbed his wrist and took his pulse, which didn't concern him. Then she'd started to question him. Silly questions at first. Like asking him what time it was, and asking him to describe Seattle's weather. But then she'd started asking him about his work. And the questions kept coming. And even though some part of him knew that he shouldn't answer, both for everyone's safety and because of attorney-client privilege, he answered anyway. Completely. He told her *everything*. He even handed her his TRAC security card, and told her how to operate the computers. And told her where the cameras were at TRACE. He even gave her the

TRACE security code, for Chrissakes! 'Why did I do that?'

Standing, he almost falls backward into bed again but manages to stumble over to the window. Looking out, the grounds are green and well-maintained. An ornate fountain that looks like it belongs outside a Spanish villa is hemmed in by perfectly manicured shrubs, all of it surrounded by grass and lined with young maple trees around the outside. Just beyond them, however, the lawn and trees give way to desert. Some two hundred yards beyond that a series of large white metal structures, perhaps airplane hangars, loom. There are dozens of them. In the space between, maybe a hundred yards out, a large sign says something he can't quite make out at first. Squinting to read it, he thinks it says "Medal of Freedom Manufacturing Facility, Haliburton Corp."

Making his way to the bedroom door, he opens it, entering a grand great room. What appears to be a curated collection of prints, pictures and flags lines the walls of the room, each with a matching gold frame. Some of these are certificates related to the launching of IPOs, awarded to "Original Shareholders," including for Haliburton Corporation, BridleChem, the Saudi Binladin Group, HRG Group and Zapata Petroleum Corporation.

Between these the prints and pictures include an image of the famous, some would say *infamous*, "Mission Accomplished" ceremony held on the USS Abraham Lincoln at the supposedly "victorious" end of "Operation Iraqi Freedom," led by a former United States President. A few others are of his former presidential father, including his shaking hands with the King of Saudi Arabia and the President of Afghanistan, and being awarded the Presidential Medal of Freedom by Barack Obama. Rounding out the collection is an assortment of miniature flags, including of Texas, Kuwait and the shortly-waved Desert Storm Flag. There's also a caricature of disgraced Iraqi dictator Saddam Hussein with a noose around his neck, signed in the lower righthand corner by the artist.

He's leaning in to try to figure out what one of the prints is, realizing that it's the burnt remains of a comic book, when the door at the far end of the room opens, and in walks the former President himself, flanked by two large men wearing navy blue suits, crisp white shirts and blue-and-red-striped ties. Suddenly it dawns on him, the name he'd occasionally heard whispered over the years, and all the rumors of oligarchic 'masters of the universe' planning global domination during orgies in the redwoods of Northern California, ending in blood sacrifices. He'd thought most of it absurd when he'd heard such things; the lunacy of conspiracy theorists given credence by a public desperate for the sensationalism confused with truth.

"Ah! *Arbusto*! I get it now! Spanish for..."

     The House on Apple Blossom Lane

The former U.S. President winks and places his forefinger over his lips: shhhh. "I know. You expected a Mexican. Puppets and pawns, counselor, puppets and pawns. Distracting showboats and sacrificial chess pieces, nothing more. Many of them are deadly, yes, but there's a snake charmer for every snake, Mr. Mills. Or as they say here in Texas: Don't kill the gopher snakes, they keep the rattlesnakes from overrunning the ranch."

Gesturing for him to sit, the two suits moving into opposing corners of the room, Jonathan Mills falls into the brown leather chair beside the fireplace opposite his host. 'What a chair,' he thinks. 'Feels like power.' Opposite him, the look on his hosts' face says it all. 'He's got that same stupid grin he had throughout his presidency,' Jonathan thinks. 'The look of a kid that gets everything he could dream of every Christmas, and imagines that he was born into deserving it.'

"My dad always used to say that this is the greatest country on Earth, Mr. Mills. A place made for the cowboys. The wildcatters. The only country in the world where a man can fully realize his worth."

"Okay…"

"You're just such a man, I think. The people I work with think the same. But you were playing a very dangerous game, Mr. Mills. And I hope you understand that we were compelled to remove you from the playing field before your coach benched you, permanently. If you catch my meaning…" His shit-eating grin somehow grows broader.

'He thinks he's clever,' Jonathan thinks, holding back a grin of his own. 'He's definitely not doing the heavy lifting in this operation. The same had to be true of his presidency.'

"What matters is that you're playing for the *right* team now. So your children are safe.

They should all be here soon. And my associates tell me that your former employer shouldn't be an issue, but I think we should keep y'all here for a while, just to be safe." He walks over to the window, staring towards the series of immense white metal buildings in the distance. "After all, this is one of the very places that makes sure America *stays* the greatest country on Earth. What better place to plant your own flag, eh, counselor?"

Jonathan Mills thinks about for a minute. He realizes that he doesn't feel any greatness. He only feels defeat.

"As long as you're sure we're safe from Carpenter…"

"Another Epstein, the papers will say. The Haldol will be chalked up to the security guards swearing to his being out of control. As to how he got ahold of a belt and why the security cameras malfunctioned, none can say." Still grinning ear to ear, the trademark bemused look glued to his face, Junior walks back over to his seat, plunks himself down and, suddenly serious, says: "Now, Mr. Mills, let's talk about your future. *Our* future."

Only a few miles away now, Duncan is completing his own journey. Between the sedative and having already been physically, mentally and emotionally exhausted even before he was drugged, the all-day-and-night cross-country drive goes by like a blur. Sleeping through most of it, Duncan is vaguely aware of the extent of the southeastern escapade, through areas of the country that he's never before seen, the green gradually losing ground to brown. Even in the more lucid moments the events of the previous days are jumbled. The interrogation at the police station seems like a dream; and the creeping sense that Marie is the boogeyman is its nightmarish post-script.

The sun is setting as the Escalade crosses the border. "Welcome to Texas," the sign says,

"Drive Friendly – The Texas Way." The iconic single-white-starred, red, white and blue Texan Flag seems to Duncan as though it's declaring their passage into a foreign country. Sitting up in the spacious, black leather backseat, endless questions collide in his mind, all battling for his attention. But as Marie removes her sunglasses and glances at him with those icy blue eyes through the rearview, he loses the will to ask her.

Stretching, he hears a crinkling sound. Something awkwardly fills the right front pocket of his jeans, the same pants he'd been wearing the day before. Marie had thought it prudent not to have him shower or change, and to add another half-dose of the Lorazepam to the water she had him drink. Waking him after returning from her early morning work, she'd led him out to the vehicle more asleep than awake, plunking him down in the backseat, already pillowed and blanketed.

Reaching in and retrieving the envelope, he stares at it blankly. It takes him a full minute to realize what it is, even after reading what's written on the outside. It's the coffee-stained envelope that he'd grabbed in those chaotic moments in the secondary unit of 6160, as its occupants burned alive. Opening it and pulling out the three crumpled white sheets, they catch Marie's eye.

"What is that, Duncan?," she demands.

Ignoring her, he begins to read:

On TRAC 2020: Strategic Summary

April 1st, 2020

For executive eyes only – TRAC NDA in effect

Increased stringency by the FDA as to the permissibility of human trials for new pharmacological products has imposed increasing costs and product testing and development delays for our clients. At the same time, animal testing has not yielded sufficiently reliable results or actionable information as to which products warrant FDA application for human testing, as too much deviation exists between animal and human model results. Moreover, financial, temporal and logistical costs increase even more when the products requiring testing impose a significant health risk for trial participants. Yet the potential benefits of products demand testing.

"Duncan, I asked you a question."

With the sheer demand for new products for both the public and private sectors, including for defense applications, it has become necessary to find alternative means to initiate preliminary human trials that may yield the necessary information as to which products hold the potential for formal FDA trials and approval. In exchange for services rendered to vulnerable, insolvent populations, product testing is warranted. Mentally ill populations hold the advantage of conferring significant levels of reasonable doubt for the induction of product testing applications. The mental and bodily state of said participants is both unsound and unstably in flux, thus allowing for the incorporation of potential side effects induced by new products without raising red flags, or with those flags able to be taken down (so to speak) through the creative use of psychiatric terminology of partner practitioners in order to conceal the cause of symptoms, thus allowing for the continuation of product testing at low legal risk.

"Where did you get that, Duncan?," she demands with more urgency.

The populations served by TRAC confer the added benefit of offering countless subjects whom mirror the symptoms of our surviving soldiers returning from overseas incursions. Thus are we competitively positioned to garner invaluable data on the psychological deprogramming and reconditioning necessary for the fostering of more reliable, resilient soldiers. As defense funding continues to climb at a record pace in our current conflict-rich geopolitical climate, under the table demand for product testing also continues to increase.

Through covert channels, DARPA has enticed its pharmacological partners to develop drugs which augment the amenability of trainees to deep conditioning programs, as well as to find reliable, repeatable means to induce amnesia when unwanted effects are incurred.

Contraindications, adverse events and side effects may be readily classifiable as professionally diagnosed preexisting and emergent symptoms of mental illness, and as purposefully triggered re-visitations of past traumas per the exposure and desensitization theory of trauma treatment.

Marie reaches back with her right hand and grabs for the papers, but Duncan pulls back just in time. She pulls over to the side of the highway. He reads as fast as he can.

It's also advisable that COVID be taken advantage of to further the aims of TRAC projects, utilizing both its lower-lethality 'common contagion' form as introduced by our client in Wuhan (so as to conceal testing source and motivation), and in its more lethal derivative forms, as means to mitigate the risks and conceal the causes of unsuccessful testing. While the targeted spread of 'common COVID' yields invaluable data in terms of public epidemiological studies, especially via transoceanic proliferation, as well as lucrative inoculation sales opportunities, the weaponization and control values of the more lethal derivatives of the virus per future international conflict resolution should not be underestimated. TRAC is supremely well-positioned to profit from the expanded scope of said studies.

Even only vaguely comprehending the implications of what he's reading, Duncan's heart drops further with every paragraph. As Marie comes around the left side of the Escalade to open his door, Duncan leaps across the seat to the other side and is out the opposite door, sprinting into desert.

In addition, for clients moving illicit substances both domestically and internationally in the meeting of ever-increasing domestic demand, TRAC offers unprecedented insulation. The legal protections and concealing fronts formed by cost-subsidized public universities paired with support by our pharmaceutical partners and the goodwill engendered by mental health and trauma treatment permit low-risk means of trafficking. Even with suspicion from law enforcement, substances may be easily camouflaged through pharmaceutical product lines and mental health treatment regimens. Connected business concerns also permit ideal laundering conditions.

He's been fast-walking away from her, through sand and scrub brush. Tripping over a purple-flowering cluster of strawberry hedgehog cacti, he nearly face-plants into the red-bulbed center of a horse crippler cactus. Sitting up and turning around, Marie remains in pursuit, but unhurriedly. She knows her prey can't escape. Seated in the sand, he finishes his father's document.

Finally, by establishing international operations offering free health services to impoverished populations residing in areas of narco-production, we both build goodwill with residents and government, further facilitating the low-risk efficacy of our operations, and thicken the smokescreen in the eyes of competing and conflicting parties. Thus is a reliable international network currently under construction connecting charitable outposts south of the U.S. border, and soon in the Middle East, to TRAC's going concerns in the U.S. Through the expansion and solidification of this network, and through the purchased fealty of select, strategically-targeted partners, TRAC aims to be beyond reproach.

- *Jonathan Mills, TRAC Chief Counsel*

As he finishes the letter, Marie snatches it from him. Quickly flipping through the pages, she grins first, then laughs lightly, shaking her head. Pulling a silver torch lighter from her pocket, she ignites one edge of the three crinkled sheets. Going up in flames, she throws them to the wind. Reaching down to Duncan, she calmly offers him her hand.

He's done fighting. He takes it.

The End.

www.ingramcontent.com/pod-product-compliance
Lightning Source LLC
Chambersburg PA
CBHW071728150726
47998CB00005B/1556